THE PRICE OF FAILURE

THE PRICE OF FAILURE

Jeffrey Ashford

St. Martin's Press ⋈ New York

ISBN: 0-312-18156-6

First published in Great Britain by Collins Crime, an imprint of HarperCollins Publishers

First U.S. Edition: January 1998

10 9 8 7 6 5 4 3 2 1

1

Trent, a man of considerable talent, appreciated the fact that in his line of business there were occasions when success was best sought through failure. He also appreciated that a person's fears were most alarming when the mind, not the facts, set their boundaries.

He chose the team with great care, the victim with even greater. Lord Arkwright, the seventh holder of the title, had served with the Blues until inheriting the title; a man of possessions and, through upbringing and career, of controlled, predictable reactions.

Preston Later was Carolean, built in 1679, and it stood in a walled park in which roamed one of the few herds of red deer to be found south of the Border. From the point of view of security, the house was reasonably protected, but although advised by the local crime prevention officer to instal the best alarm system on the market, Lord Arkwright had settled for one that lacked sophistication. His failure to accept the advice of an expert could have been due to a reluctance to spend money – a trait of the rich – but it was more likely that he believed his record of service to his country and county would promote too much respect for him ever to suffer a criminal invasion. Like most ex-army officers from the best regiments, he could be very naive.

It took Adams just under four minutes to drill a hole through one of the three north-facing doors, to put through this a probe which consisted of a bulb –

connected by a lead to a battery in his pocket – and a mirror, both fixed on a nine-inch tube, and with this examine the inside surface of the door and its surround, to judge there was no alarm, and to force the lock. Few would have disputed his claim to be one of the smartest, quickest operators in the country.

A passage led into the kitchen. By the side of one of the wall cupboards in the kitchen was the alarm control panel; the visual display was showing 'Tap in code'. Adams knew that the standard time in between activating the alarm – which they had done when they'd entered the kitchen – and its sounding was thirty seconds; he also knew that with the system there was no passive defence. He used a small jemmy to wrench the control box away from the wall, so skilfully that there were only muted noises, and cut all the wires leading into and out of it.

They left the kitchen and went down a corridor to a door lined with green baize – Lord Arkwright, ever a traditionalist, had decreed that the separation of the two worlds was to continue to be marked even though there were now no full-time servants – and into the large hall. They climbed the wide, sweeping staircase which had heavily carved oak bannisters. On either side of the wide landing, on one wall of which hung a richly detailed tapestry depicting a stag hunt, stretched a passage. Over several days, observation had shown that lights were normally switched on in three rooms along the right-hand corridor and two along the left. They were assuming that this signified that husband and wife had their bedroom, bathroom, and dressing room to the right, their daughter her bedroom and bathroom to the left.

They moved into the right-hand corridor, then waited whilst Adams, using a stethoscope, listened at each of the doors in turn. He enjoyed acute hearing. People said that this was due to the fact that when young, he'd spent so much of his time listening to make certain his father

2

didn't find him in bed with his sister. After a while, he indicated the middle of the three doors.

They went in with a rush, torches on; the more abruptly victims were jerked out of sleep, the less likely that they would react before it was too late. Keen and Trent attacked Lord Arkwright, Turner, Lady Arkwright. Adams switched on the overhead light; he disliked violence – that was, any involvement on his part.

When the Arkwrights were bound and gagged, Trent told them what to do and what not to do, adding that their daughter would be held as hostage for their unwavering compliance. They were not to call the police. They were to have a quarter of a million pounds in used twenty, ten, and five pound notes, and be ready to hand over this money according to the instructions that would be given.

They left, switching off the light as they did so. The Arkwrights lay in the dark and discovered hell.

They went down the left-hand corridor to the first door and into the bedroom. They had Victoria Arkwright bound and gagged before she had fully comprehended what was happening.

Turner picked her up and slung her over his shoulder in a fireman's lift. During the twenty minutes it took them to leave the house, cross the park, and reach the van in a copse, he enjoyed himself immensely, running his right hand up and down her warm, firm flesh.

It never occurred to Lord Arkwright that he should keep the kidnapping secret as he had been ordered. It was his duty to inform the police. He made that point to the detective inspector who, slightly overawed by his wealth and social standing – and angry for being so – agreed. So did the detective chief superintendent from county HQ who took charge of the case. Unfortunately, neither man had sufficient imagination to see the possibility that the Arkwrights' daughter had been kidnapped not because her father was wealthy, but because his reaction to her kidnapping was virtually certain.

In view of the fact that the press must almost certainly learn about the kidnapping, the detective chief superintendent called a press conference. After giving the details, he asked the media to observe a voluntary ban on any publicity until Victoria Arkwright had been reunited with her family and fiancé. With reluctance on the part of some, this was agreed.

It was logical to suppose the kidnappers would use the telephone to arrange the transfer of the ransom money (lent by the bank at five percentage points above base rate – banks had to live). The Malicious Calls bureau of British Telecom were called in to help and they set up a constant monitor on the two lines into Preston Later and Lord Arkwright was coached on how to make the call last as long as possible without arousing suspicion. Every force in the country was asked to go on to full alert and be ready to act when the point from which the call was being made was identified.

There was no call.

The days slipped by, in normal time for most, in slow, questioning time for the police, in agonizingly drawn-out time for the Arkwrights and Victoria's fiancé. And as the days became a week, a fortnight, and finally a month, the police suffered uneasy bewilderment. Why hadn't the kidnappers demanded the ransom? Was Victoria dead? But even if she were, why were the kidnappers not trying to exact the ransom before acknowledging the fact?

At the end of the month, the police were forced to downgrade the case. However much they wanted at the very least to be seen to continue to support the family, there was no escaping the pressing demands of other and more recent cases, many just as traumatically painful to their victims and close relatives and friends.

In the early morning, two months and nine days after she had been abducted, Victoria Arkwright was bundled out of a vehicle and left on the verge of a lane in the countryside a couple of miles outside Shrewsbury. After a while, she managed to free first her wrists and then her ankles. She walked along the lane, able to see her way because it was now dawn, and reached a village spaced around crossroads. She knocked on the door of the first house and there was no answer. She knocked on the door of the second and although she noticed the curtains of one of the upstairs rooms move, once again no one responded. Desperate, overwhelmed by this indifference, she hammered on the door of a bungalow and shouted hysterically as she did so. The door was opened by a man in pyjamas and dressing gown whose initial belligerence gave way to compassion.

In hospital, she received treatment for her physical injuries and then the police were permitted to question her briefly. There was little she could tell them that was of practical importance. The several men had at all times kept their faces covered with ski masks; throughout the period of her incarceration, she had been in a small room whose sloping ceiling suggested it was in an attic, with the window boarded up so that she could not see outside. She outlined the torment to which she had been subjected in a voice so devoid of emotion it was as if she were listing the sufferings of a stranger; but the expression in her eyes made it clear that her voice was playing her false. Initially, she had been treated reasonably, experiencing only the wandering hands of the man who had carried her out of the bedroom. But after a time, and she could not judge how long because they had taken her watch, the man in command had come to the room to tell her that her father had been stupid enough to ignore orders and he had contacted the police so that she would have to suffer. And suffer she did. There were continuous sexual assaults, straightforward rape being the least appalling. Madness might have brought relief, but her mind had refused to slide over the edge; death would have brought relief, but she'd never been able to find the last ounce of willpower to kill herself.

With the case returned to the active list, the police throughout the country combed their files for men known to be sexual sadists and who might have carried out this barbarous kidnapping; every man was brought in for questioning. All without results. A psychological profile of the leader was drawn up. The psychologist postulated someone who during childhood had suffered sexual assault by a person close to him, thus destroying all sense of trust; who, however intelligent, had never been academically minded and so had been labelled backward by his schoolteachers which had resulted in his playing truant; who had discovered a natural gift for crime; who saw in violence a way of gaining respect through fear; who needed money to fund a lifestyle that would assure envy . . .

The profile would have both amused and annoyed Trent. Most of the projections were mere psychobabble, but at least one was a little too close to the truth for a man with pride.

The story could not be published in detail because by law no victim of rape could be named without her consent and no facts could be given that might enable her to be identified. But large sections of the media were past masters at providing the more salacious details of a strong story without actually breaking the law. What was written and said was quite sufficient to terrify every future potential victim and her relatives and friends.

6

Victoria left hospital a fortnight later, her body almost repaired, her mind still shockingly injured. Her mother gave her all the loving help of which she was capable, her father continued to agonize over the fact that he had been unable to help her when she had desperately needed help, her fiancé honourably, but with the shameful certainty in the back of his mind that he must fail, tried to resume their former, loving relationship.

By any standards, she had already suffered appallingly. But then came proof that while heaven has boundaries, hell does not. About the middle of her imprisonment, a newcomer had appeared to assault her, bringing fresh horror when he repeatedly told her that he had AIDS. Now, hospital tests showed that she was HIV positive.

2

Detective Inspector Hoskin stared resentfully at the pile of files on his desk. Police officers were being turned into clerks by the demand for paperwork – a case could call for 50, perhaps even 100 forms to be completed, signed, checked, countersigned . . . How many trees were felled simply because someone, somewhere, wanted to be seen to be important?

There was a knock on the door and Detective Sergeant Wyatt stepped into the room. 'Ian's just called in, Guv.'

'And?'

'By the time he got there, the bird had flown.'

'Shit!'

'He questioned the mother, but couldn't get anywhere.'

'Why not?'

'She's a bit soft in the head; or makes out she is. Seems all she'd say was that Lenny left home yesterday evening and said he wouldn't be back for a couple of days.'

'She didn't ask him where he was going?'

'If I had Lenny living in the house and he said he'd be away, I wouldn't ask any questions in case he changed his mind.'

'What about known contacts?'

'He's a brother living on the other side of town, but he's straight and so there'd be no joy there. Ian's sniffing around the pubs and betting shops, hoping to find someone who can help.'

'I want him brought in fast. There are those four other

break-ins with his hallmark. With the evidence we've got this time, he's nailed, and that should persuade him to cough the others and they can be taken into account.'

Confirmation, Wyatt thought, that the DI's willingness to spend time and resources on a relatively minor case was due to the chance of clearing up several with one arrest. The monthly clear-up rate was due to be calculated soon; the last set of figures had not favoured the division.

'Anything else on the books?'

'A hit-and-run just beyond Altingham has just come in. The victim has a broken leg, but nothing more serious.'

'Can he identify the car; any witnesses?'

'No witnesses and he was far too shaken to get the number; he says it might have been a red Volkswagen, although on the other hand it might have been a Vauxhall.'

'Great!'

'Then we've had a punch-up on the Richard Mann estate, but that was quickly calmed down and the two men brought in and cautioned. The front desk has had old Ma Tower reporting another man in her house – one day she'll strike lucky and there actually will be one. And that's about it.'

Hoskin looked at his watch. 'All right.'

Wyatt turned, pulled the door open, checked. 'I nearly forgot. A woman rang in to complain of a heavy breather on the line; and he's been active for a bit. I told her we'd get in touch with British Telecom's Malicious Calls bureau and ask for their help.'

'Send someone along in the morning to have a word with her, more as a PR exercise than anything, since there's probably nothing we can do until BT reports.'

'Will do. 'Night, Guv'nor.'

Totally predictable, Hoskin thought. Middle aged, nearing his retirement with almost thirty years' service, unambitious, conscientious to a degree . . . The perfect detective sergeant for an ambitious detective inspector who was too busy watching his front to have the time to watch what was happening behind him. He yawned, locked his fingers and cracked the bones – something which made Miranda squirm – and stared at the telephone with sharp dislike, as if blaming it for the call he had received earlier. Jack Warren. Lucky bastard! One of his off-duty D Cs, dragooned into shopping with his wife, looks across several racks of clothes to see Cooney Jackson who'd been on every force's wanted list for the past six months; Jackson, always boasting he could smell a split from a mile away, for once too occupied with a blonde to notice what's happening until it's happened. So Detective Inspector Warren of C division has a high profile wanted in his hands just when promotions are being discussed at county HQ. And this when E division's clear-up rate is falling, as the detective chief superintendent has mentioned a couple of times . . .

He stood, crossed to the ancient coat stand and lifted off his mackintosh. He left, looked in at the CID general room to check who was there, continued along the corridor to the lift. It seemed only fitting for a day that was ending sourly that the lift should be at the ground floor and seemingly determined to stay there. He carried on to the stairs and went down, trying to gain meagre consolation from the fact that he was taking a little of the exercise that both Miranda and the doctor claimed he needed.

He crossed the courtyard to the blue Mondeo, unlocked it, and settled behind the wheel. For no particular reason other than ill temper, as he started the engine, he remembered that the monthly repayments on the car were due the next day. And once again, he'd failed to win the lottery.

The twenty-minute drive took him past the railway station, through the depressing area of terraced houses of south Everden, and out into the country. Fourways Farm was a late-Elizabethan farmhouse, set in the middle of fields which belonged to the farmer who had sold the

10

house away from the land. It had the typical long roof that had once provided the outshut, peg tiles, variegated bricks, two inglenook fireplaces, one with benches and recesses for warming mugs of ale, exposed beams by the score, and, so the agent had said, an occasional benign ghost. On their first viewing, Miranda had moved from room to room with the look of a woman who was already placing the furniture.

Later, on their drive back to the modern, characterless house in west Everden – which no ghost would bother to haunt – he had pointed out that they'd set themselves a limit of a hundred and fifty thousand, which would use up a not inconsiderable part of her aunt's inheritance, and the asking price of Fourways was two hundred and ten thousand. Her reply had been typical Miranda. The agent had indicated that a quick sale would be welcome and so an offer of two hundred thousand would probably succeed; budgets were guides, not tablets of stone; by the time they'd redecorated, removed some of the so-called improvements, and got the garden how she'd have it, the property would be worth two hundred and twenty thousand, so they'd have bought a bargain. And, of course, it was her dream house. She was a genius at arranging facts to suit her wishes.

He drove into the double garage and parked alongside her battered Peugeot 205. He'd suggested more than once that she used the Mondeo and he the Peugeot because she had to do so much more driving than he, but her reply was always the same – provided a car went and stopped when she wanted, she didn't care what it looked like. He was fairly certain that her attitude to life led some people to believe her a snob, but in fact she was both determined and shy and it was this shyness that was responsible for their misjudgement. Far from striving to keep up with the Joneses, she didn't give a damn what they were doing or saying. Her reason for wanting Fourways Farm had not been because a country cottage was chic, but because from the moment she'd walked into the hall it had been

11

welcoming and promised her and her family happiness. (She believed all houses developed character; beware of living in a hostile one.)

He left the garage and went down the gravel drive to the thorn hedge which encircled the garden, still colourful despite the month. As he opened the wooden gate – he'd promised to repair it; he would when he had the time – he recalled their first meeting. The force's annual ball, held at county HQ in Rickstone, all ranks invited, but only those who could behave welcome . . . By chance he'd been introduced to the chief constable's wife. She'd been a pleasant woman (unlike the present chief constable's wife, who seemed to be understudying royalty) and had chatted for a while before introducing him to the daughter of friends whom her husband had invited . . . Love at first sight. The sophisticated laughed at it and until then he'd regarded it as a useful ploy to get a romantically inclined woman into the sack. But he'd fallen in love with Miranda during their first dance . . .

Her parents, relatively wealthy, had never said so to her, far less to him, but he was certain that they'd always hoped she would marry someone from a similar background to theirs, not a mere detective constable . . . It was this certainty which forever fuelled an already sharp ambition. He was determined to make high rank before they died.

She met him at the front door, kissed him hullo, said she'd bet he'd never guess whom she'd met that afternoon, then gave him no chance to win or lose her bet. 'I came face to face with Madge at Boots.'

'Madge?'

'Madge Sexton.'

'Should I know her?'

'You really are hopeless when it's not work,' she said with good-humoured resignation. 'The parents live near the Sextons and Bill and I were like brother and sister. He married Madge Parsons and after the wedding I didn't see them again until that day they called in here on their way back from Dover. You must remember – we were picking the Bramleys and wondered who on earth we knew who owned a Bentley.'

'I remember the Bentley, but not . . . Or was she the woman who looked like she'd just been frightened silly?'

'At school we used to call her Parsley Tops because her hair was always such a mess.' She ran her fingers through her lustrous black hair that held a natural wave and almost always looked as if it had just received expert attention. 'I asked them back here, but they were on their way to the Continent and had only stopped off in town to see if Madge could buy something she'd forgotten. She told me they've bought a house near Auch.'

'Wouldn't Monte Carlo have been more their scene?'

She linked her arm with his. 'Why so gritty? Has it been a hard day?'

'Bloody frustrating.'

'Then come on through and I'll get you a drink.' She uncoupled her arm, led the way into the square sitting room which had so low a central beam that he had to duck under it. 'What's the order, sir?'

'G and T, please. And if your hand slips while pouring the G, don't panic.'

She crossed to the very short, narrow passage that lay between the central brickwork of the back-to-back fire-places and the north-facing wall, opened the cocktail cabinet that stood there.

He sat. 'Where are the kids?'

She appeared in the doorway. 'Ellen asked them over to play with her two and promised to run them back.'

'She's a glutton for punishment. Wasn't it the last time that they were together that they all fought like Kilkenny cats?'

'That was then, now's now. Which reminds me. I remembered earlier on that you've only five years left.'

'To do what?'

13

'To become chief constable.'

'You wouldn't be rushing things, would you?'

'Then you don't remember promising me you'd be C C by the time you were forty?'

'A man'll say anything to get a woman into bed.'

She laughed, disappeared. A moment later, she stepped back into the room, a glass in each hand. She put these on the occasional table by his side, leaned over and kissed him. 'Would you like to know what really got me into bed with you that first time?'

'My irresistible sex appeal?'

'Your woebegone expression after you and Father had had your little chat.'

'It wasn't woebegone, it was disbelief at being forced to behave like a nineteenth-century berk and list all my credits and debits because I'd proposed to you.'

'I'll bet the debits took a heck of a lot longer to recite than the credits.'

'Which shows how little you know me.'

'The little I do know, I like.' She kissed him again, straightened, moved to the armchair on the other side of the table, sat.

He studied her. A connoisseur would probably criticize the depth of her forehead, the high arch of her eyebrows, the thrust of her nose, and the size of her full, moist lips, but surely could find no fault in her deep brown eyes that sometimes expressed her emotions more clearly than she wished, or in her figure that would have been a credit to a younger woman who had borne no children . . .

She half turned to face him. 'A penny for them?'

'Will you have them expurgated or interesting?'

'I thought you were so tired.'

'Not that tired.'

She was in bed and he was changing into pyjamas when she said: 'What's gone wrong today?'

'Mostly a lot of little things.'

14

'Such as?'

'Minor villainy that we won't be able to clear up and the clear-up rate will suffer.'

'But there's nothing major?'

He stepped into the pyjama trousers, walked round the bed, climbed in. 'Not long before I left the station, I had a call from Jack Warren. Officially, he was asking for the expedition of some cross-border cooperation, unofficially, he was gloating over the fact that one of his crew nicked a villain that the whole country's been looking for for the past six months.'

'Which means a feather in his cap?'

'A whole bloody peacock's tail. And you know what? It wasn't smart coppering, it was sheer sodding luck!'

3

Carr left the bus and walked the two hundred yards to divisional HQ, hurrying because the drizzle was beginning to turn into icy rain. Gloria's brother lived in Sydney and every letter from him was filled with sunshine, golden beaches, warm sea, and why didn't she persuade Mike to emigrate? Perhaps in Australia, she would not have been confined to a hospital bed . . .

He entered the ten-storey concrete and glass building and made his way up to the CID general room on the fourth floor. Illness, injuries, and courses, had reduced numbers and only one other DC was present.

'How's the missus?' Buckley asked.

'Much as before.' He threaded his way through to his desk, sat. He was not a man who usually talked about his misfortune, but was grateful for the chance to do so now. 'If only they could move her back to the maternity ward it might do some good, but they say they can't because she's become long term and they have to keep all maternity beds ready for immediate occupation.'

'It's a real bugger having kids. You'd have thought that whoever arranged things would have made it easier, like it is for the kangaroos.'

'I don't suppose women would welcome walking around with their kids in pouches until half grown.'

'I suppose there's a point there . . . Any news when they might let her out?'

'Not until the baby's born.'

16

'And there's no knowing when that'll happen, except that it'll be in the middle of the night. Makes it rough for her.'

'Even rougher when she keeps getting someone in the next bed who's either gaga or who pops it. Doesn't help her depression to have someone carried off feet first.'

'I can imagine.'

'I've asked around to find out what it would cost for her to go into a private nursing home as she so wants.'

'What's the answer?'

'Not all that short of five hundred a week. Where does a copper find that sort of money?'

'Not in his pay packet.'

'So it's not on. And every time I go there and see her getting more depressed and know that if I had the money . . .' He became silent.

'I can imagine.'

Could he? Carr wondered. Could he even begin to appreciate his feelings of pity and self-condemnation as he tried to lift Gloria out of her latest bout of depression and to convince her that this pregnancy would go to full term and she would finally bear the baby she so desperately wanted?

Buckley said, happy to change the conversation: 'The skipper was shouting for you.'

'What's the panic?'

'Can't say.'

'Then I'd better find out.' Carr stood, left, and went along to the detective sergeant's room.

'How's Gloria?' Wyatt asked.

'Not too bad.'

'Freda wants to know what she really likes most, fruit or chocolate?'

'Chocolate, but she has to keep off it because she must keep her weight down and that's hell when she's not taking any exercise.'

'Any particular kind of fruit.'

17

'Everything but figs. Apples as much as anything.'

'I'll tell Freda to find some Coxes. Trouble is, most of the shops are filled with those French apples that don't taste. The only thing the French are good for is garlic.'

In many respects, Carr thought, Wyatt was the archetypal John Bull. Likely to complain that it was impossible to understand the natives in France because they all jabbered away in French.

Wyatt opened a folder, picked out a single sheet of paper. 'We had a complaint in yesterday, too late to do anything; you can deal with it now. As the guv'nor said, more of a PR job than anything. Miss Genevieve Varney, Flat 3, Easthill House, 36 Egremont Road. She's been getting dirty telephone calls. We've advised the Malicious Calls bureau so there's not much more we can do at the moment, but you can ask a few questions to make it seem like the whole division's been put on the job. And if she's the usual middle-aged, dried-up spinster, don't overlook the possibility that she's making the whole thing up.' Then he said, with studied casualness: 'I suppose that address isn't far from the hospital.'

Which meant, Carr understood, that a quick visit to see Gloria afterwards would go unremarked. He left and returned to the general room to collect his mackintosh. Wyatt came from a breed of coppers that was dying out fast. His creed was stolid loyalty for and to the unit. And loyalty meant fostering the regimental spirit (to many, a concept fit only to be jeered at) and being prepared to be concerned in problems that lay beyond work. Normally, he would demand that rules be observed on the grounds that they were rules; but if someone within the unit needed help, then that observance might take on a flexible air. Which was why he'd dropped the hint about the nearness of the hospital . . .

Carr stepped into the general room. 'D'you know if both CID cars are out?'

'Couldn't say, mate,' Buckley replied. 'What's the news?'

'Only some woman who's been receiving hot telephone calls.'

'Seems like more and more people are getting their kicks in strange ways. Makes you wonder if being normal isn't odd.'

Carr went down to the courtyard and found that one of the CID Escorts was parked there. A good omen? Perhaps Gloria would have cheered up since the previous evening. He sat behind the wheel, started the engine, backed out, turned, drove to the exit and waited. The traffic did not thin and as his impatience grew, he suffered an abrupt swing of emotion. It was a shitty world! The hospital staff were competent and caring, but the endless pressures of their jobs left them unable to appreciate the unique problems of individual patients. 'When you're with her, try to be more cheerful. Laugh and joke,' one of the doctors had recently said to him, almost as if prescribing a dose of ipecacuanha. Did the stupid bastard think he spent his time with her detailing all his own woes and miseries? Couldn't any of them understand that however illogical it was for her to be so affected by conditions in the ward, since they were by most standards good, if they did depress her with an ever-growing intensity, then logic had no part to play . . . And on top of his fear and vicarious suffering, there was the added pain of knowing that could she be moved to a nursing home, she might slough off her depression whether this was logical or illogical. He'd tried to find the money by raising a second mortgage. But the building society had been very quick to point out that their house had become trapped in negative equity by the falls in value of property. So Gloria was condemned to remain in hospital because he'd no other way of raising the money to be able to move her. In bitter contrast to his position, each day there were reports of politicians putting up their pay above the rate of inflation, of incompetent directors being given platinum handshakes, of City workers expecting Christmas bonuses that would ensure they kept drinking champagne, of sportsmen earning hundreds of thousands on the final putts, even – and bitter irony here – of servicewomen being paid fortunes for having become pregnant . . . An oncoming lorry stopped. He flashed the headlights as a thank you, drove on to the road. Reason returned. All right, life wasn't fair, but that was hardly news. Adam had discovered this truth when Eve had cajoled him into eating the fruit of the tree of knowledge of good and evil. All her fault, but he'd been just as severely punished as she.

The area around Bullock Common, named after a mid-nineteenth-century philanthropist, had once been the smartest part of Everden and the houses reflected that fact – large, three-storey Victorian and Edwardian buildings with the blunt, forceful character of the age. Even now, when the motor car had caused so much to change, it was still a road suggesting prosperity. He parked between a Volvo and a Mercedes.

Number 36 had a small, well-tended front garden. He passed through this, climbed the three steps to the front door, checked the name tags on the entryphone unit, pressed the button for flat 3.

'Who is it?'

The loudspeaker had distorted the voice too much for him to make even a guess at the speaker's age. 'Detective Constable Carr, divisional CID. Is it convenient to have a word?'

'Come on up.'

The door lock buzzed and he entered. The hall was large, but sparsely furnished and the flowers in a vase on the table were looking distinctly tired. He climbed the two flights of poorly carpeted stairs and as he stepped on to the top landing a door opened and Genevieve said: 'Hullo.'

So much for Wyatt's dried-up, middle-aged spinster! She was in her early twenties. Her figure was outlined, but not too closely defined, by sweater and jeans. Jet-black hair framed an oval face in which the most noticeable feature was large, deep blue eyes; her complexion was peaches and cream, her nose impishly inclined, her mouth shapely and only a muscle twitch away from a smile. She made him think of his lost innocence.

'Do come in.' Free of the tinny distortions of a loud-speaker, her voice was soft and warm.

He followed her across a small hall into a large sitting-room, furnished in modern style, which offered a view of the common.

'Will you have a drink?'

'Thanks, but no thanks.'

'Then it's true! Policemen on duty don't drink.'

He returned her smile. 'Not before midday.'

'Do sit.'

He sat, waited until she was seated on the settee. 'What can you tell me about the phone calls?'

'Not very much, I'm afraid. Now I just put the receiver down when I know it's him.'

'When was the first?'

'I suppose it was roughly three weeks ago.'

'Yet you've only just reported them?'

'There was a break after the first one and I hoped he'd gone away. It's only in the last few days they've become such a nuisance. As a matter of fact, I've been making a note of dates and times – would that be of any use?'

'It might very well be.'

'I'll get it for you.' She crossed to a small table on which stood a phone and answerphone unit. She opened a notebook, brought out a loose sheet of paper, handed this to him.

He briefly studied the dates and times. There was no readily discernible pattern to suggest the caller had some sort of routine. 'What has he said to you?'

'What you'd expect.'

'Could you be more specific? If some of the words embarrass you, just use some sort of symbol, like X Y Z.'

'I'm not embarrassed – after all, one hears them on the

21

television all the time – it's just that I don't like speaking them.' She looked anxiously at him. 'Does that sound really stupid?'

'Far from it. It's how my wife thinks.'

'Then here goes.' She repeated what the caller had said.

'Fairly standard, I'm afraid.'

'I can't think why anyone should behave like this.'

'After another case recently, I asked a psychiatrist if he could explain. He waffled on about the man suffering a dominant mother which left him frightened by the power of women and unable to form normal relationships with them. The calls give him the chance to revenge himself by humiliating a woman who doesn't have the chance to reject him. For my money, psychiatrists would bring in mother love-hate to explain why a chicken lays an egg.'

'Are they dangerous?'

'Psychiatrists?'

She smiled. 'The people who make these calls.'

'Very unlikely. What they're after is to be able to talk dirty without running any risks.'

'It's just . . . Well, I've been wondering.'

'He won't offer any physical harm,' he said authoritatively, even though this was not strictly certain. 'Now, as to what we can do to help. We've been on to British Telecom . . .'

'They've phoned to say they'll be along as soon as possible. In fact, I thought you must be the engineer.'

'Good. I expect they'll instal one of those gadgets that tells you the number of the caller. And also an alarm unit that you'll activate if the call unit is blank because the man's used the withholding code; as I understand it, they can still trace his call. But I'd better point out that it may not help all that much to trace where he's phoning from because if he's any sense, he'll use a public box. In which case, there'll be precious little chance of directly identifying him. Probably the best bet will be for you to ask BT to change your number and have the new one ex-directory . . .'

'I can't do that.' She noticed his look of inquiry. 'I do a little work from home and can't afford to be cut off from my clients.'

Clients could be advised of the alteration, he thought, but did not pursue the point. 'Then we must try to identify the caller indirectly. If you can think of anyone who might be pestering you, I can have a word with them . . . You say the first call was about three weeks ago. Just before then, did you have a row with anyone?'

She thought back, her brow slightly creased. She shook her head.

'Did anyone make a pass at you which you smartly rejected?'

This time she smiled briefly as she again shook her head.

'Did you have any workmen in?'

'I haven't had any men in for months . . . Hang on, that's not right. The phone went on the blink and an engineer came along and fixed it.' She hesitated, then said: 'And as a matter of fact, he . . . I was going to say something that's probably very stupid.'

'I doubt it.'

'It's just that he was a bit of a creep and made me think that a lot of nasty thoughts were going around in his head. But it's absurd to judge from appearances, isn't it?'

'Mostly, but not always. Did you learn his name?'

'I'm afraid not.'

'Did he actually say or try to do anything unpleasant?'

'Not overtly. But although he'd never look directly at me when we were talking, I did once catch him staring at me with a look that made me feel I needed a bath. Does that make any sense at all?'

'It does. When exactly was this?'

'A month back, give or take a couple of days.'

'In other words, before the first obscene call?'

'That's right.'

He stood. 'I think I've covered everything. We'll do all we can and I'll be in touch.'

She led the way to the front door and as she opened it he noticed how the sweater tightened to outline her left breast . . . He jerked his gaze away. He wasn't a randy teenager. But as he made his way down the stairs, he realized something of which he must have been aware almost from the moment of meeting her, but which he had not consciously acknowledged until now. She possessed all the charm of innocence; but also, however contradictory this might seem, a vibrant sexuality that stretched a man's imagination.

4

Carr drove into the hospital forecourt and, since the time was outside official visiting hours, had no difficulty in parking. He climbed out of the car, turned and stared at the central building which, despite a very expensive facelift, still looked more former workhouse than hospital and was in such stark contrast to the two modern wings.

He remembered the past in a series of flashbacks. On Gloria's first ever visit, he'd taken time off to accompany her, as confident as she that all was going well, despite the fact that their GP had decided the visit was necessary. How could anything be wrong when she was, apart from some morning sickness, feeling on top of the world? A blood test had shown that either something was seriously wrong or the baby was dead; a scan showed it was dead. Pregnancy had been too advanced for an abortion and she had had to suffer an induced labour. As much as he'd tried to share her trauma, only she knew exactly what hell it had been — bringing forth death not life. The hospital had been unable to cite any cause for the death of the baby. She'd suffered from depression, but soon overcome it because she was a strong-willed woman. Her second pregnancy had ended in the same way, except that since she was only eleven weeks pregnant, she had had an abortion. This time, the hospital had discovered that she was suffering from pre-eclampsia, a condition which, if unchecked, could develop into eclampsia, putting her as well as the foetus at risk. They'd told her that now they could treat her, any future pregnancy should be successful. Should be, not would be. It had taken him weeks to help her lift herself out of the deeper depression following this second loss and to believe in 'would' not 'should'. Her third pregnancy had raised both her hopes and her fears, but thanks to the treatment of hormone injections and a low dose of aspirin, for a long time it was all hope. Then, suddenly, her blood pressure had risen and there had been a dangerous increase of protein in her urine. The hospital had told her that she must become a temporary in-patient in order that the closest possible watch could be kept on her condition and extra treatment be given immediately if this became necessary. Abruptly, fear replaced hope; fear so strong it overwhelmed her, bringing in its train a depression considerably deeper than those she had previously suffered. And with this depression had come the conviction – which to everyone but she was illogical – that if she remained in the hospital where she had suffered two losses, she must inevitably suffer a third. No argument on anyone's part could shake her conviction . . . One of the specialists had called him into a staff room for a 'chat'. His wife was in so depressed a state that there were fears that her physical condition might be affected by her mental, with the potential result that all the treatment might be negated. It was to be hoped, the specialist had continued, that he made every effort to be cheerful when he visited her and did not burden her with his own tensions. It was, of course, difficult for the husband to be deprived of his wife when the marriage was relatively new, but it really was up to him . . . The specialist would have been surprised to learn how Carr had silently been describing him.

He reached into the car for the bag of peaches, shut the door and locked it. The doorman inside the main entrance did not stop him because this was outside visiting hours, but nodded a greeting – there were some advantages to being a policeman. He took the lift up to the fifth floor and

26

went down the long passage to Hampton Ward. The duty nurse gave him a professional smile, said: 'The latest scan shows that everything's fine.'

'That's great. Has it cheered her up?'

'For a while, but . . . I'm afraid she was very upset when she heard that a woman she'd met in here has just had twins.'

Twice the bitterness of another's success. He had learned that there would be no point in his now trying to get her to see things in a normal light; she could only view them subjectively. He walked between the beds, watched by the other women. Not so long ago, one of them had complained that he was allowed to visit his wife outside the usual hours and had refused to accept that his work with all its irregular times was a good reason. When he'd heard this, he'd silently cursed her for her bloody-mindedness – then had learned that her boyfriend had not visited her once.

Pregnancy and illness had not been kind to Gloria. It had aged her, adding lines and slackening flesh. He kissed her, put the fruit down on the bedside table, sat on the chair and held her hand. Sometimes she'd remain virtually silent, wrapped up in her own world; sometimes she'd talk with frenetic energy as if so little time were left; sometimes she'd behave normally and he'd find himself hoping that she'd overcome the worst, even while experience suggested that his hope would prove to be false. 'The nurse says that the scan shows everything's fine.'

'That's what they always say.'

'Hugh asked me how you were and said that women ought to be like kangaroos and have babies too small to bother about. But as I pointed out, what woman's going to want to carry junior around in a pouch for the first few years?'

'That's better than not having anyone to carry.'

Nought out of ten, he thought, for leading into that one in an attempt to lighten her mood. 'Trish rang to find out how you were.'

27

'So what did you tell her?'

'That everyone's hopeful things will be fine this time.'

'Everyone? You'd better tell the specialist, so that he knows.'

'Love, the last time I spoke to him, he said that there's no reason why you shouldn't very soon have junior bouncing on your knees.'

'If he thinks that, why's he always so bloody miserable?'

'Because his wife is a terrible cook.'

She didn't smile, but she did change the subject. 'Are you eating properly?'

It was usually a good sign when she worried about him rather than herself. 'Like a fighting cock.'

'But you must have finished the food I put in the deep freeze?'

'I'm indulging myself. Last night I had duck and orange from Marks and Sparks.'

'Was it good?'

About to say it had been delicious, he checked the words. Too much enthusiasm and she might think that he wasn't missing her cooking. 'Not bad, but a little pricey . . . How are you doing for books?'

'They came round yesterday.' She indicated two books on the bedside table. 'The bottom one starts off with a baby dying.'

Life had never heard the old tag about never kicking a man when he was down; perhaps life was, in truth, sexist. 'What about the other one?'

'I've only read the blurb. It's set in the Highlands.'

'Just so long as it's not written in a Scotsman's idea of English. I've always wanted to see the Highlands. What say that as soon as possible we drive up north and show them to junior?'

'If you like.' She stared into the distance for a while, then focused her gaze. 'Have you seen Anne and Andy?'

'Not yet. They've twice asked me to a meal and each time I've had to call off at the last moment.'

28

She suffered another sharp change of mood. 'It's such a beastly unsociable job.'

It was an old and universal complaint.

'Freda says it can only get worse,' she added petulantly.

'If she means with promotion, that's probably true as far as detective inspector. After that, it's county HQ and rumour holds that up there the only people who do any real work are the tea ladies. Talking about which, I'd better make a move.'

'You've hardly been here any time.'

'I know, but I'm not meant to be here at all. It's only because a job turned up nearby and Sean was a brick and made certain I had it.'

'He's a kind man.'

'One of the best, provided you play things straight.'

'Freda told me how much he's looking forward to retirement.'

'My guess is that it'll be a lot more than she is. He'll upset her routine if he's around the house all day long.'

'Won't he try to find a part-time job?'

'There aren't many of those around these days, not for men his age. In any case, given the chance to vegetate or work, he'll vegetate. He's always talking about the joys of sitting by the river and staring at a fishing line.' He stood. 'What's the order for my next visit – grapes, oranges, bananas?'

'A kilo block of Cadbury's Dairy Milk.'

'I wish I dare, love, but if I did bring that, the nurse would have my nuts.'

She said bitterly: 'Why the hell is it that as soon as one can't have something, one wants it all the more?'

It was a question that must have tormented her many times. He bent down and kissed her, whispered words that made her smile for the first time and briefly restored her looks that pregnancy and illness had stripped away.

He walked the length of the ward, spoke briefly to the sister who was standing by the desk, and carried on down the corridor to the lift. As he waited after pressing the call button, he remembered what she'd said about wanting. It seemed half a lifetime since they had made love.

5

As Carr left the room, Wyatt thought that there went a man who might or might not make the grade. People who joined the police force from a sense of public service that was touched with idealism had always been at risk; in the modern climate of selfishness and disregard for others, they were very much more so. Law and justice had drifted further apart, the trust between citizen and police had all but vanished, there were dozens of charities committed to defending the rights of criminals, but only one to support the victims of those crimes, the left wing did all they could to destroy existing society by maligning the police at every turn, and this was aided by the media, but it was impossible to turn the clock back. One could only retire.

The internal phone rang. The DI wanted a word. There was one man, he thought, who was going to make the grade, but only time would tell if it would be as high as he coveted. He was no idealist, being far too ambitious. Half-remembered lines from long ago schooldays briefly floated through his mind. Ambition was a grievous fault, grievously answered for . . . The DI would never accept that.

He went along the corridor to the DI's room. Hoskin was bundling papers into a briefcase. 'I have to steam up to county, so you're holding the fort for the rest of the day. Anything fresh in?'

'Nothing that need detain you. I've put in hand the two witness statements that A division is yelling for.'

'When you send them on, add a note that we've better things to do than spend all day clearing up their work for them.'

'I'll do that with pleasure.'

The DI briefly looked at him as if wondering whether he could be so stolidly unimaginative as to think that that had been meant seriously. He resumed putting papers into the briefcase.

'There is one thing, Guv. Carr's had a word with Miss Varney about the heavy telephone calls. The Malicious Calls bureau have said they'll set up the equipment and so if chummy rings from a private address, we'll have him. If he's a shade smarter than that, there's not much to go on apart from the fact that just before the calls started her phone went wrong and the engineer who mended it struck her as being distinctly dodgy.'

'Hardly a good lead. A sizeable proportion of the population looks definitely dodgy.'

'There is the coincidence of the times.'

'Did you ask Carr for his assessment of the woman?'

'His description is, she'd get a hermit hopping.'

'Not many hermits left these days . . . How's his wife?'

'The child's still alive, but her depression doesn't get any better; worse, if anything.'

'Must be like hugging a time bomb . . . I may or may not look in on my way back; depends what time I manage to get away.' As he finished speaking, the phone rang. 'You answer. I left a couple of minutes ago and right now am driving out of the car park.' He left in a rush.

Wyatt lifted the receiver. 'Wyatt, CID.'

'It's Miranda Hoskin here, Sean. Is my husband around?'

'He left for county just before you rang, Mrs Hoskin. Is it important?'

'No, not at all . . . How is Freda and the family?'

'Very well, thanks. Evelyn's having a child.'

'That's wonderful news. She must be very pleased.'

32

'Delighted.' But Bill, her husband, was less so, having recently been made redundant. Despite the good screw he'd been making, they hadn't a penny saved. The modern generation . . .

'If you see my husband, you might be kind enough to ask him to ring me at home.' She said goodbye, rang off.

He always found her manner patronizing; the squire's wife making an effort to be sociable. Freda called him an old fool for thinking like that; Miranda Hoskin was more genuine than a lot of DIs' wives and he was mistaking shyness for superiority. Freda might be right. She usually was.

Although Wyatt had never thought in such specific terms, he accepted that in order fully to appreciate something, one had first to be deprived of it. Because as a boy he had lived in a back-to-back with small, dark, damp rooms on the walls of which had grown fungus and which lacked both bathroom and indoor lavatory, every time he drove into Meansworth Crescent and came in sight of number 16, he felt a glow of happy pride. Although an unremarkable semi-detached, number 16 was for him Buckingham Palace and Edinburgh Castle rolled into one.

When they'd married, it had been the policy of the force that officers lived in police housing, rent free. Years later, that policy had changed and officers were then encouraged to buy their own houses and to help them to do so they had been given a housing allowance; those who had not wished to make the change had been allowed to stay on in the police houses, but had been reminded that on their retirement they would have to leave and find other housing, and that would not be easy in view of the reduction in the number of council houses and the existence of left-wing councils who would take great pains to find reasons for failing to provide accommodation for retired policemen. Freda had accepted the idea of buying a house with enthusiasm, he had havered. It had been she who had found that they could obtain a semi-detached in north Everden if they used almost all their savings to meet the initial ten per cent deposit of the purchase price – the minimum the mortgage companies would accept at that time. Initially, he had refused to consider the possibility. Their savings were the buffer between them and the world he had suffered when young; they owed not a penny and weren't going to put themselves into debt they might never be able to repay. Again and again she'd argued that a mortgage would merely be transferring their savings from one form to another; that after he retired, his pension would enable them to keep up with the payments until the house was theirs; that they would be able to leave the two girls something worthwhile . . . She was middle aged and normally far from pushy, but when she wanted something for her family she was prepared to battle her way around the moon and back to get it. She'd badgered him, braved his resentment at this badgering, and even out-faced him when, for only the second time in their marriage, he'd lost his temper and verbally assaulted her. And it was right after he had shamefacedly apologized for all he'd said – and had suffered additional shame because of her immediate forgiveness – that he had suddenly understood why the thought of purchasing a house had always panicked him. When he'd been young, there had been a terrible row between his parents over money and debt and his father had struck his mother, then stormed out of the house. He had crouched under the kitchen table, trying to hide from the catastrophe called debt which had overwhelmed them . . .

Six weeks later, number 16 had become theirs.

All the houses had been built without garages because then it had been inconceivable that those who lived in them could ever afford to run cars. He found a parking space, locked the doors, walked along the pavement, opened the wrought-iron gate, and continued through the small front garden – immaculately kept, as was the back garden; both Freda and he were keen gardeners – to the front door. As he stepped inside, Jane came out of the front room. 'Hi.' She passed him and went up the stairs. Brief as the greeting had been, it was more than he sometimes received. Relations between them were never as smooth as had been those between Evelyn and him. Jane made a point of nonconformity. Recently, she'd become friendly with a man with an outrageous hairstyle and earrings. Pure yob. All right, one couldn't forever swim against the tide, but that didn't mean one had to paddle in the backwaters of a sewage plant . . .

Freda appeared in the doorway of the kitchen at the end of the hall. 'Evening, love.'

He went forward and kissed her on the cheek. She'd lost her looks and her figure, but he still saw her as the woman he'd married. 'What's for grub?'

'Steak and kidney pie. It'll be ready soon, but there's time for a drink if you'd like one.'

'That's the best idea I've heard all day.'

He followed her into the kitchen, crossed to the larder. 'D'you want a lager, or something else?'

'A lager'll be fine.'

He opened and emptied two cans, stepped back into the kitchen, handed her a glass. They drank, for a while not talking because they had long since reached the point where they could be comfortable with silence. Then he wiped his mouth with the back of his hand. 'Mike popped in to see Gloria this morning. Says the baby's still alive.'

'How long's she got to go now?'

'He didn't say. Can't be long, surely?'

'I keep praying she'll make it.'

He knew that that was literally true – she did pray. He didn't because he'd seen too much of the underside of life to believe in a loving God. But that didn't worry him because he never questioned the reason for his existence, being content merely to accept it.

She put her glass down on the kitchen table, went over to the stove and checked the contents of the two saucepans. 'Cauliflowers were cheap, so I bought one. You like them, don't you?'

'That's right.' There were other vegetables he preferred, but long ago she'd got it into her mind that cauliflowers were one of his favourites and he'd never thought it worth the effort to contradict her.

'Eve rang earlier. She thinks Bill's found another job.'

'Surprised he could summon up the effort to look.'

'Stop talking like an old man, Father. It's Eve that's married to him, not you or me, so how he goes about things is for her to worry over.'

Bill always made a fuss of her. 'Is Jane in for grub?'

'I don't know.'

'She ought to say.'

'It won't make any difference to what's on the table whether she is, or isn't.' She turned back from the stove, studied him. 'How's the day been?'

'Much as usual, really.'

'Something seems to have got to you.'

He drank. 'The Old Man's been sharp enough to cut himself.'

'What's upset him?'

'Jack Warren, over at C division, has pulled in a villain the whole country's been after for months. That'll have him smelling of violets at county. Which could scupper our Bevis's chances of promotion.'

'He'll surely get that sooner or later?'

'I reckon. Tell you one thing. I hope to hell I'm retired before he's wielding real clout. Blokes like him make life bloody difficult for the rest of us.' He drained the glass, belched.

'I keep telling you not to do that.'

'What's it matter when neither of the kids are around to hear?'

6

As Carr walked into the general room, Atkin – the newest member of CID and still finding his way around – said: 'The telephone people rang through just now and said to tell you that Miss Varney has had another obscene telephone call and it went on long enough for them to trace it.'

'And?'

'The number's listed under the name of Mrs Dunn and the address . . .' He looked down at a sheet of paper on his desk. 'Oakley, Torrington Without. I asked him, without what?'

'And no doubt he congratulated you on your wit?'

Atkin grinned.

Carr looked at his watch. 'I'll run out there now and find out what's what.'

'D'you need back-up?'

'Yeah. I've a load of G forty-fives to complete so the job's yours.'

Atkin swore.

Carr entered his forthcoming journey in the Movement Book, kept on the table under the notice board, then made his way down to the courtyard and the CID Escort.

He could easily have passed through the village and not noticed it. There were only half a dozen houses and bungalows stretched out on one side of the road. A village that lacked a pub? On his return, he could tell Atkin why it was called Torrington Without.

In the garden of the end bungalow, an old man dug with the endless rhythm learned from the days of farming before full mechanization. Carr stopped the car, leaned across to lower the passenger window, and asked where was the house called Oakley? The old man dug another spit, straightened up slowly, hawked and spat, and, leaning on the handle of the fork, stared into the far distance. Carr waited, understanding the country character sufficiently well to know that any sign of impatience on his part would arouse scornful amusement.

'Turn right after Ebb's Wood,' the man finally said.

Carr drove on, past fields hedged with thorn and down to winter corn, and reached a small wood that was being coppiced; it was interesting, he mused as he turned right, how some of the old ways of farming were returning in an attempt to work with Nature rather than against her.

Because it seemed probable that Oakley was where the caller – Mrs Dunn's son? – lived, he had subconsciously been expecting to find a house as mean in character as the obscene calls. Reality was a large gateway with elaborate gates flanked by curving brickwork and beyond which – though only the several chimneys could be seen above the trees – lay a large house. Had Atkin, over enthusiastic as ever, misheard at least part of the name of the house? Oakley Cottage? . . . He drove through the gateway, passed a range of buildings to the left that clearly had been stables and accommodation for the outside servants and when the drive forked, chose the left-hand side. It looped around the trees and bushes to bring him to a large, sprawling Edwardian house that was far more imposing than it was attractive.

He parked by the raised circular flower bed, left the car and crossed to the porch which would not have disgraced a minor palace. The massive wooden door was patterned with wrought-iron studs and the bell pull was in the shape of a fox's head. He waited to be greeted by the traditional butler who, with one superior, snide glance would indicate that he should have used the tradesmen's entrance. The door was opened by an elderly woman with a face of rough-hewn granite who appeared to be dressed in cast-offs.

'Yes?'

'Detective Constable Carr, county police. I'd like a word with Mrs Dunn, if she's in?'

She moved to one side and he accepted this as an invitation to enter.

She pulled the door shut with a quick squeal from the massive iron hinges. 'What d'you want?'

'If I could speak with Mrs Dunn . . . ?'

'Who the devil do you think I am?'

He hoped the answer wasn't obvious. 'I'm here concerning a telephone call . . .'

'I've not made any call to the police.'

'It was to Miss Varney . . .'

'I know no one by that name.'

He persevered. 'Nevertheless, Mrs Dunn, this morning someone phoned Miss Varney . . . Is this house the only one called Oakley?'

'Of course.'

'Is there an Oakley Cottage?'

'No.'

'Then the call must have come from here.'

'Nonsense.'

'There was a trace on Miss Varney's line and . . .'

'A trace? . . . I've never heard such ridiculous nonsense.' Without warning, she turned on her heels and stumped across to one of the four doors which led off the very high-ceilinged hall. He followed her, wondering as he did so who had shot all the heads mounted on the walls?

The room was large enough to contain a grand piano that merely took up one corner. Through the three wide, deep windows, there were views across gently sloping land to the distant sea.

'Kindly explain what you are talking about, young man.'

Ten to one she was the local master of foxhounds and God help any would-be hunt saboteurs who tried to upset her sport. 'Over the past three weeks, Miss Varney has received a number of obscene calls. She reported that fact to us and we got in touch with the Malicious Calls bureau of British Telecom who put a trace on her line. At around eleven this morning, there was another obscene call and BT have informed us that it was made from this address.'

'Are you suggesting that I made the call?'

'Of course not, that's unthinkable,' he hastily assured her. 'But I imagine you have staff?'

'Vera. There is no one else.'

'Does she have a son or any other male relative who either lives here or has recently visited her?'

'She's unmarried and dislikes all her relatives.'

'Do you employ outside staff?'

'There's Andrew, the gardener. A damned good worker, unlike his predecessor who spent half his time sitting on his bum.'

He all but giggled because he found it surrealistically amusing that she should use the word 'bum'. 'Might he have been in this house some time around eleven?'

'Most unlikely.'

'But you can't be certain?'

'My good man, since I do not have him in view all the time, of course I cannot.'

'Were you at home?'

'I was in town, trying to deal with the incompetence of my bank.'

'Was Vera here?'

'Yes.'

'Do you think I might have a word with her?' He thought that she was going to refuse, but in the end she marched out. He stared round the room at the strange and confusing contrasts it offered. The curtains were faded, the

40

armchairs and two settees needed re-covering, one of the two carpets on the parquet floor was noticeably threadbare, but a third one, with a triple medallion design, which hung on the wall, was in pristine condition and glowed with colour, two bow-fronted display cabinets held small, beautifully crafted figurines, and three paintings of pastoral scenes possessed a quality that made him certain, despite his ignorance of art, that they were worth a great deal of money.

She returned, accompanied by a woman who was dressed neatly and with some taste and whose expression was placid.

'Well, ask,' snapped Mrs Dunn, as she thumped down on the nearer settee.

He faced Vera. 'Can you say whether the gardener was in the house this morning at around eleven o'clock?'

'He came in for his coffee like always, but that was earlier.'

'How much earlier?'

'Half-nine, like as not.'

'And he was in the house for how long?'

'A quarter of an hour; never stays any longer.'

'Did he return later on?'

'No.'

'Are you sure?'

'Couldn't be more certain.'

Initially, he was surprised by the almost aggressive confidence with which she had answered the last question. Then he reflected that to work for Mrs Dunn, she must possess a stronger character than was immediately apparent. 'Has any other man been in the house?'

'Only the telephone engineer.'

'Why was he here?'

'We've had trouble with the line crackling and going dead. I asked 'em two days ago to do something about it and it took them until this morning to turn up.'

'What was the time when he was here?'

She thought. 'Must've been around eleven.'

'Was he on his own?'

'Well, I had to look to the cooking.' For the first time, she was unsure. She looked very quickly at Mrs Dunn. 'I thought it would be all right, leaving him to do the work. I made him show his identity card before I let him in.'

Eureka!

7

Chance sometimes leads to farce, but more often to tragedy. Had Trent not left number 36 as Carr was walking towards it . . .

Trent was a conceited man, yet at the same time smart enough to recognize his own weakness. He held the police in contempt, but accepted that there were a few who were smart and therefore he always allowed all of them a greater degree of intelligence than he believed they possessed. So during the course of a job, he invested in self-denial. He enjoyed wine, especially a Chambertin or, if feeling like a millionaire, a Romanée-Conti, but since even a couple of glasses could affect a man's judgement and Sod's law decreed that that judgement would be most needed when least available, he became a temporary teetotaller; he no longer had a woman living with him, even though his sex drive became still greater because of the tension, as women were emotionally unstable and not to be relied upon. Instead of wine he drank Coke, instead of a live-in woman, he bought the pleasures of really high-class tarts who were the soul of discretion. The first deprivation was a penance; the second could have its advantages.

Eros would have watched their performance with pride. At the conclusion, he handed Genevieve an envelope and she accepted it without counting the money it contained. He had been very generous. Not only did that generosity do his self-esteem good, it was fair reward for the touch of genius she brought to her work.

'Come back soon; real soon,' she said, with soft inviting warmth.

There were times when it was all too easy to believe that she really did find him so attractive that she loved him for himself, not his money. He reminded himself that she was a Tom, not a loving companion. Yet as he walked down the stairs, he found he was working out how soon he could visit her again. He silently cursed. From now on, he'd confine his attention to Yvette. She might lack the final sophistication – there was no air of innocence wherever she was – but he never found any difficulty in thinking about her with contempt.

His silver Porsche 911 Carrera was parked a couple of hundred yards down the road. That car was the one ostentatious possession he allowed himself; his one public statement that he was no erk. One day, when rich and beyond the possibility of trouble, he'd buy a Ferrari 456 GT. Then would the herd envy him!

Once in the car he started the engine and revved it hard for the pleasure of hearing it snarl its superiority.

Carr was too far away to make out the features of the man who came down the steps of number 36 and walked off in the opposite direction, but because the other came from the house to which he was going, he automatically noted the short-length, fawn camel's-hair overcoat. A smart dresser. And as the other reached a silver Porsche, Carr added rich to that description. He heard the engine being revved too fiercely before the car moved off. Some survival yuppie who hadn't learned from experience.

He climbed the steps of number 36 and pressed the top button on the entryphone unit. After a while, he pressed it again. Finally accepting that she was out, he turned and was about to descend to the pavement when her voice came through the loudspeaker. 'Who is it?'

He returned and spoke into the microphone. 'Detective Constable Mike Carr.'

'I'm sorry to take so long. I was in the shower.'

It would have needed a purer mind than his not to picture the scene. The door buzzed and opened to his push.

She met him at the entrance to the flat, wearing a towelling bathrobe and looking as if she were advertising bottled freshness. 'What fun to see you again! Come on in.'

He entered and closed the door.

'Will you wait in the sitting room while I slip some clothes on?'

'Roger.'

'And do have a drink this time.'

'Perhaps I could pocket my halo for a short while.'

'They say it's more fun to be a sinner than a saint.'

Who was going to argue with that when she was around? He went through to the sitting room, settled in one of the armchairs, picked up a magazine and leafed through it.

When she entered, she was wearing a blouse and skirt, had tied her hair into a ponytail, and hardly looked old enough to have left the convent school. 'What would you like – gin, whisky, brandy, sherry, Cinzano?'

'Would you have a lager?'

'I'll try and find the kind that reaches all the parts.' She left.

She wouldn't have realized that what she'd said was capable of a double meaning, he decided.

She returned with a tray on which were a filled glass, an empty glass tumbler, and an unopened can. She handed him the tumbler and the can, crossed to the second armchair, sat.

He pulled off the tab, poured out the lager. 'I wanted you to know as soon as possible that I'm reasonably confident I've identified the telephone pest who's been bothering you.'

'You must be a miracle worker.'

'Just lucky. The Post Office traced the call you heard earlier and it came from a private address. I've seen the people who live there and to cut a long story short, they have been having trouble with their telephone and an engineer went along to put things right and he was in the house, unobserved, at the time of the call.'

'And he admits it was him?'

'I haven't questioned him yet and won't until I have confirmation from BT that he was the engineer who fixed your phone as well. Not that I've any doubts really. Just as you did, the housekeeper described him as unctuous, oily, and no painting. So with any luck, you won't be bothered again.'

'I think you're wonderful!'

He grinned. 'I wish my boss agreed with that.'

'He doesn't?'

'He'd criticize an archangel.' He finished the lager with practised ease, stood. 'Sorry to rush, but I'm aiming to nip into the hospital to see my wife for a few minutes.'

'She's ill?'

'Unfortunately, a very difficult pregnancy which means she has to be under constant skilled care to head off trouble.'

'I do hope everything goes all right for her.'

'Thanks.'

'It's very kind of you to take the time to call in to tell me the news. I'll sleep a lot more easily tonight.'

If he were around, she wouldn't get much sleep . . . Since he would be seeing Gloria in a few minutes, it was just as well that wives didn't have the ability to wander around inside their husbands' recent thoughts.

8

Morrell had intended to take the train down to London, but he was absurdly superstitious and when the second black cat crossed his path from right to left, he knew that disaster was waiting for him and hurriedly returned to the house in south Bishops Retton. There, he did indeed find disaster. Nick was in bed with another man in what polite society called a close embrace. Far from showing any sense of shame at this betrayal, Nick jeeringly told him to take a walk round the block so that the two of them could finish in peace. Normally a man who eschewed violence, Morrell grabbed an empty beer bottle that was on the floor, intending to smash it on the head of the newcomer. But he was inherently slow and clumsy and before he could deliver the blow, Nick had rolled off the bed and dug the blade of a flick knife into his stomach.

Initially, he was convinced he was going to die, despite the hospital's assurance that he was not, but after a while he began to take heart. He considered what had happened and came to the conclusion that the painful course events had taken had largely been his fault because he had allowed his immediate emotions to overwhelm his common sense. He'd always known Nick was promiscuous, but since he had never previously had to face the reality of this promiscuity, he had relegated the knowledge to that part of his mind where unwanted truths were concealed; Nick's wanderings had always been of a temporary nature, searching for novelty, not stable relationships, and therefore everything would once more be all right provided his prickly pride was assuaged. Morrell wrote a letter of apology that would not have disgraced the pen of Uriah Heep. Two days later, a scrubber who looked as if she'd started to draw the old age pension arrived at his bedside and said that Nick had given her a tenner to come and pleasure him when the nurses weren't looking. The insult was so brutal, it made him cry.

It was sheer good fortune that the detective constable from K division arrived at the hospital before Morrell's tears had finally dried.

'Had any second thoughts?' demanded the DC roughly, not bothering with any form of greeting. If one man could epitomize the macho culture of all police forces, it was he.

'What d'you mean?' Morrell mumbled.

'D'you still want to claim the knife wound in your guts came from slipping and falling on a toothbrush?'

'It was a piece of wood that was sharp, like.' Morrell struggled to overcome his grief. 'Honest, that's the way it was. You've got to believe me.'

'Believe you? I'd as soon believe a politician. But I don't give a tinker's toss. It's my guv'nor who's a bit soft in the Ted and reckons you ought to be given the chance to name the knifer so as he can be hauled before the courts on a charge of cruelty to animals.'

'I slipped and fell.'

'So next time don't wear such high heels.' The DC turned away.

Morrell took a deep breath. 'Inspector.'

'Haven't you heard that they've made me detective chief superintendent?'

'I could tell you something interesting.'

The DC turned back. 'How interesting?' His tone was now crisp, not contemptuous.

'Like finding who did the Arkwright job.'

He tried to hide his sudden excitement under the cover of overt scepticism. 'You think I'm that soft I'll believe a mob that heavy would let you near their shadows?'

'It's like I know someone who's in with 'em 'cause he's tops in his job.'

'You're full of shit.'

'We had a relationship.'

He sat on the next bed, which was empty.

'A real deep friendship.'

'Sounds cosy.'

'Only I got home to find him . . . With another relationship.'

'Leave out the amusing bits.'

'I'm only trying to explain.'

The DC remembered the need for subtlety. 'You go right ahead and explain.'

'It's when things were still all right. Before the . . . We'd been out on the bottle and when we got home we had some more. He was talking big and said he'd soon be travelling around in a Lamborghini. I laughed. That got him shouting, on account of us both having had a skinful. You know how it goes.'

'I've been told.'

'He swore he was in on another job and this time it was going to make millions because the family'd do exactly as they was told on account of being so shit-scared after what had happened to the Arkwright woman.'

'What's his name?'

'I ain't saying. I ain't no snout. It's only on account of me feeling sick over what happened to that young bit. I wouldn't want to see that happen to anyone else.'

'The feeling does you real credit.' Normally, the DC thought, Morrell wouldn't give a damn if a dozen young women were raped and infected, so what was his real motive for talking? Revenge? What better way of gaining that than by shopping his former companion? But to do so directly would identify himself as the informer and if he

49

did survive such an identification, it would only be as a permanent cripple. So do everything indirectly. Provide information that would harm his late lover, but in circumstances that did not incriminate him. And if this meant that the rest of the mob might also be netted, tough ... Quite suddenly, this had grown far too big for him to handle. The detective inspector should take over. But instinct suggested that very recently something more had happened to scramble Morrell's emotions to such an extent that temporarily he had only the one thought in his mind, to get his own back on the man who had betrayed him. If now there were any pause – which there must be if the DI were to be called to the hospital – there had to be a good chance that in that time Morrell's emotions would calm sufficiently for him to think clearly, in which case he must refuse to say anything more ... The DC decided to gamble and not to call the DI, knowing that while he might be putting any future promotion on the line, he might stand the chance of helping to prevent another woman from suffering a hideous ordeal. 'Your friend was in on the Arkwright job, then?'

'That's what I said.'

'Who heads the mob?'

'He's never told.'

'No nicknames?'

'Nothing.'

'When's this next job?'

'Soon.'

'How soon?'

'Couldn't say.'

'Who's the victim?'

'He ain't never given a name.'

'There could be real money for solid information.'

'I swear I've told you all I know.'

The DC paused to consider the situation. Morrell must know that he had to give more information if the police were to have anything to go on. So why was he withholding this? Because he wanted to have it forced out of him so that he could not blame himself for giving it? To accept that was to take another gamble, since threats might frighten him into silence rather than provoking him into speech . . . Another gamble that had to be taken. 'You're saying too much and too little.'

'How d'you mean?'

'Too much for us to ignore it, too little to give us anything to work on. Frustrating. Know how some coppers react when they get frustrated?'

Morrell ran his tongue along his fleshy lips.

'I'll tell it straight. They get real impatient, especially those with kids. Like as not, they start playing it rough.'

'They ain't allowed to touch me.'

'If they all stick to the same story, the judge will believe 'em when they say you fell over a chair. Reminds me of the bastard who claimed he'd no idea who'd shaken his little kid's head so violently, her brains had scrambled. He broke both arms and a leg falling over a chair.'

Morrell moved uneasily and gasped as pain sliced through his stomach. The D C stood. 'Play it your way, then.'

'He . . .'

'Yeah?'

'He did say something more.'

'So name it.'

'This new job was a cert for millions on account of the father being a pop star who'd give anything to get his kids back.'

'Kid or kids?'

'He said, kids.'

'Where do they live?'

'He never said. You won't tell no one I've talked, will you?'

Given his way, the D C would have shouted the news from the rooftops.

9

Every police force in the country was asked to identify any highly successful pop star who lived in their territory and who had two or more daughters, probably in their teens.

It became apparent that self-styled successful pop stars littered the countryside, but the qualifications eliminated almost all of them; only a handful were truly successful and only three of them chose to live with the daughters they had fathered.

The police visited each of the three and explained that his daughters might be at risk and advised how best to meet that threat. One had an immediate nervous breakdown, terrified that in any kidnapping he might suffer serious injury.

Trent was a criminal by choice, not through circumstances. A rebel from childhood he had grown up to despise conformity, to view every civilized barrier as something to be breached, and to believe that his rejection of every standard that enabled people to live together in harmony to be a sign of his superiority. He approved of Nietzsche.

That he had dangerously absurd views on some subjects did not prevent his regarding others intelligently. Normally, only a brief watch needed to be kept on an intended mark because normally that was sufficient. But when playing for maximum stakes, it was only sensible to take maximum precautions and he had given orders that from the beginning Inchmoor House should be kept under close surveillance. An incipient mutiny – most criminals were averse to regular, boring work – was quelled and watch was maintained either from the crown of the small hill that lay in front of the huge mid-Victorian mock castle, or from the woods to the side.

At ten-thirty on the 11th December, Rathbone, cursing the light drizzle which had started half an hour before, saw a light van turn into the quarter-mile-long drive lined with elms which had escaped the disease that had killed so many trees over the past years. He pulled the binoculars from their case and cursed again as a sudden swirl of wind splattered drizzle over the lenses, distorting images. By the time he had cleaned away the damp, the van was parked in front of the fifteen-foot-high porch. He could just make out the lettering on the side. Security experts. Two men unloaded the van and carried several boxes of varying sizes into the house.

A small white saloon car came up the drive and parked alongside the van. A man in uniform climbed out, adjusted his peak cap, crossed to the front door. He was admitted into the house.

Time passed. A Volvo estate arrived and after it stopped a woman and two girls left it and crossed to the front door. The woman was wearing a very short skirt and he kept the binoculars trained on her. She could move into his day-dreams any time.

Trent drove down to the coast and parked on the broad sea wall – stone-faced on the sea side, grass on the top and shore side – that ran for several miles. He left the car and walked into the westerly wind which plucked at his hair and at the lapels of the leather bomber jacket, carrying with it the salty smell of the sea. A couple of seagulls, squabbling over something, reluctantly rose as he neared them and let the wind take them up and away. He reached a moth-eaten tennis ball, abandoned by some summer visitor, and repeatedly kicked this ahead until he sliced it over the edge of the wall and into the grey, sullen sea that was at high tide.

He came to a stop and stared out to sea. On the horizon, blurred because of poor visibility, was a supertanker, bound westwards; nearer inshore, a coaster was scending surprisingly heavily in what appeared to be only a very moderate sea and swell. He was thankful not to be aboard her; he was one of the world's worst sailors. He jammed his hands into the pockets of the jacket to keep them warm.

The evidence strongly suggested that security at Inchmoor House was being stepped up from a previously already high level. Why? Had the police been called in to advise because the owner realized how at risk his family were? If so, it was mere coincidence that this was the target house. Coincidences occurred almost as frequently as non-coincidences. But it could prove fatal to assume it was coincidence because such an assumption was so much more acceptable. The police might for once have pulled out their fingers and drawn up a list of all the families in the country who were most at risk and were now advising them to take the extra measures necessary to protect themselves. The family in Inchmoor House would certainly figure in any such list. Or had the police somehow learned that this was the target for the second kidnapping . . . ?

He resumed walking, finding in movement a help to thought. How to determine if the police had, against all the odds, had a tip-off? He put himself in their place. His advice would be first to add to the defences of the house with the most sophisticated devices that money could buy, secondly, to recognize that the intended kidnapping might well take place somewhere other than in or around the house. The two daughters were taken to, and brought back from, school each day either in the Rolls with the personalized numberplate or the Volvo. The Middle East had in the past shown that if well organized, a kidnapping from a car was relatively easy. So it would be common sense to employ a couple of bodyguards. Then the appearance of bodyguards would surely prove, as clearly as was likely to be possible, that there had been a leak . . . He came to a stop, his expression savage, his fists clenched. If there proved to have been a nark, he'd use piano wire to throttle the bastard so slowly that he made the trip to the fires of hell a dozen times before he died.

On the 12th December, two men accompanied the mother and daughters in the Rolls and another two followed in a Mondeo. If you were seriously rich, you could buy yourself a private army.

Trent accepted that only a halfwit would now go ahead with the kidnapping, yet he suffered the urge to do so, not only because he hated losing, but also because if successful he would prove himself so much cleverer than they. In the end, common sense prevailed.

The kidnapping of Victoria Arkwright and setting up the second kidnapping had cost big money; now that the latter had to be aborted, finances were in danger of becoming decidedly unhealthy. In addition, the team were becoming restive, unsettled and beginning to wonder if he were not quite the winner they'd believed. Good reasons for quickly finding a new target. But a nark would betray their next target, as he had betrayed this one . . .

Was there a nark? Previously, he'd argued that there must be because the family would only have employed bodyguards if told that they were the intended target. But clearly it was possible that having been warned, his family, along with others, must consider themselves a possible target, the father had on his own account hired bodyguards . . .

As intended, the Arkwright kidnapping had shocked the country; it was this sense of shock that was designed to secure success without a hitch for the second kidnapping. But time, in an age when television screens were filled with tragedies every day, quickly dimmed even the most horrific event. So he had to move quickly. But he had to know the truth before he moved. How to discover what that truth was?

10

Even the most convoluted problem had a solution; the only problem was discovering what that was.

Frustration of a non-sexual nature always had the ironic effect of increasing Trent's libido; it was as if failure in one sphere led him to turn to another where he could dominate. After hours spent in trying and failing to decide conclusively whether his plans had been betrayed by an informer, he decided he needed a woman. Yvette, who reduced events to their primary nature? Yet whatever he'd promised himself previously, it was Genevieve who could offer him the illusion . . .

Afterwards, they lay on the bed and relaxed. Genevieve never hurried her clients, knowing that this distinguished her from the average tart who begrudged every wasted moment.

She broke the silence. 'Do you remember the last time you were here?'

He didn't bother to answer.

'You'd no sooner gone than the detective called.'

'After the Lord Mayor's coach . . .'

She moved until she could lie partly across him, breasts on his stomach. He had a hairy chest and she began to twirl hairs into spirals. 'He told me he was almost certain he'd found out who was making the dirty calls; one of the telephone engineers. Only he hadn't spoken to the man yet, so he couldn't be absolutely certain.' She created another two spirals of hair. 'I wonder what kind of satisfaction he gets?'

'From being a copper?'

'No, the telephone engineer. I feel sorry for him.'

'Why?'

'His wife's in hospital.'

'He's got to get his satisfaction somehow.'

'I'm talking about the detective. She's pregnant and something's wrong so she has to stay in hospital.'

He wasn't interested in other people's problems; he had more than enough of his own. And now that his passion was assuaged, at least temporarily, they came flooding back. How to make certain whether or not the police had been tipped off? Did he really have to find the answer? Could he skate round the problem by not disclosing to the others who their next target was until they actually set out to do the job? . . . Only if he was prepared for them to go in blind, not really knowing what defences they faced – there might be quicker ways of getting locked up in maximum security for a fifteen-year stretch, but he didn't know what those were . . .

'Do you know Sirina?'

'Screwed her wild a couple of days ago.'

She tugged a spiral of hair. 'Silly! It's one of the Greek Islands.'

She talked about the Greek Islands so often he wondered if she saw herself as a modern-day Circe . . . Goddamnit, there had to be some way of being certain, so why couldn't he find it? The sense of frustration built up once more. He ran the fingers of his right hand down Genevieve's spine and she moved until she could kiss him as her own fingers became busy . . .

He sat up, careless that in doing so he had nearly jerked her off the bed.

'What's up? Are you hurting?'

'Shut up!' he snapped.

She lay back, her expression wary.

'This split, what sort of age is he?'

'Mid twenties.'

'And his wife's likely to stay in hospital?'

'Seems that way.'

'Then he's been starving?'

'Unless she's in a room on her own.'

'And looking at you, he must have remembered how hungry he was?'

'I wouldn't know.'

'A woman always knows if she's giving a man the hots.'

'How does it matter?'

'Did you?' he demanded angrily.

She showed no fear, even though the vicious side of his nature was suddenly obvious. 'He looked, that's all.'

'No touching?'

'No.'

'But plenty eager?'

'I suppose.'

'So if you start giving signals . . . Let's have a drink.'

She said, surprised: 'You're going to drink?'

'We're celebrating.'

'What?'

'Our partnership.'

She climbed off the bed. He watched her cross the floor and disappear through the doorway. Every movement of her body was an invitation.

She returned with a tray on which were two flutes and a bottle of Veuve Clicquot. She filled the glasses, handed him one, settled on the bed by his side. 'What partnership?'

'The one that makes you ten Ks.'

'For doing what?'

He dipped his finger in the champagne, rubbed it on her right nipple. 'For reminding a detective constable that he's still got balls.'

Her father had died when she was five and her mother had taken to the bottle in a big way, leaving her all but abandoned; she might have featured in a sentimental

59

Victorian music-hall song. Her aunt, who'd run a high-class call-girl system for many years with both taste and tact, had removed her from her mother's care and virtually adopted her. Life had been lived in a spacious flat, attractively furnished because her aunt was a woman of considerable taste, and she had attended a school for young ladies, highly recommended by one of her aunt's regulars. On her fifteenth birthday, her aunt had given her a diamond and ruby brooch and then initiated a woman-to-woman talk. 'You know I love you as a daughter and therefore I want the very best in life for you, so it's time to look to your future. When you've finished at school, you can go to university, but ever since they opened Oxford and Cambridge to the hoi polloi they no longer offer social advantages, only disadvantages. You can become a model, but as much as the idea may attract you, I have to say that you are not sufficiently bitchy to reach the top. We can find you a rich man to marry, but rich men are so uninteresting and mean . . . My dear, I have not the slightest doubt that your future lies in exploiting to the full your unique talent. You know what I mean, of course?'

'I don't think I do.'

'Your ability to look at one and the same time like an innocent virgin and a woman for whom sixty-nine is more than half of a hundred and thirty-eight. I've often wondered from whom you've inherited so priceless a gift. After all, my natural assets are unambiguous and my poor, dear sister cannot be said to have had any at all. There is, of course, no need to make up your mind yet. One should always be extremely wary of men who seek to go too far down the road of youth. Eighteen will be time enough.'

On her eighteenth birthday, her aunt had given her a diamond necklace and had introduced her to a stockbroker who had paid a thousand pounds for the pleasure. That evening, she had taken her aunt to dinner at the Ritz as a small thank you for all her kindnesses.

She had been nineteen and a half when a man so rich that even head waiters bowed and scraped had taken her for a month's cruise in the Mediterranean on his hundred and fifty-four foot yacht. One day, they'd anchored off the island of Sirina and she had discovered heaven . . .

She had instinctively liked Carr, admired his concern for his wife, and did not wish him any harm, but there was always a point at which emotions had to give way to practicalities. Trent had raised his offer to fifteen thousand. Fifteen thousand, when added to her savings, meant she would be able to return to heaven.

11

As Carr shaved, he miserably wondered if there was much that was crueller than seeing someone one loved suffer and being unable to do a bloody thing about it? He went downstairs and cooked breakfast, ate hurriedly, left the house and drove to the station because on a Sunday the bus service was poor. Pettit, night-duty officer, handed over in a rush. After he'd left, Carr checked the log book, the movements book, the DI's book, the current files, and the notice board, then went over to his desk. On it, placed there by Pettit, were divisional and county memoranda, a fax from B division requiring an answer, two requests for witness statements, a photograph calling for an identification of the man whose head was ringed, papers to be filed, and a form filled in by him the previous day and rejected by the DI because of four typing errors. Fussy bastard!

The telephone rang. 'Is that Mr Carr?' a woman asked. The voice was vaguely familiar, but he could not immediately place why. 'Speaking.'

'It's Genevieve Varney.'

Into his mind came an image which he immediately blurred. 'Hullo, there. How can I help?'

'You know you told me you were fairly certain you'd identified the man who's been making those telephone calls?'

'That's right.'

'What's the position exactly?'

'As far as he's concerned? I had to rush off on another job, so one of my mates questioned him. He's denying everything and so far there's not the hard evidence to bring him in. But he now knows that we know he's the guilty man, so even if we can't take him to court right away, you won't be troubled again.'

'That's just the point. I've had another call.'

His voice expressed his surprise. 'Another obscene call?'

'Yes.'

Against all the odds, had he made a misidentification? Despite all the circumstantial evidence, was Wolf innocent? 'Was it the same man made the call?'

'I thought it was at first. But there was something different about the voice and afterwards I thought maybe it wasn't. And I put the receiver down too quickly to be certain . . . I'm scared.'

'I assure you, there's no need to be.'

'I . . . I don't know how far to believe that. I mean, of course I'm not trying to say you're a liar, but you told me only a moment ago I wouldn't be bothered again and I have been. He started saying how much more satisfying rape was than straight sex . . . That's when I put the receiver down. I'm such a coward when I think of rape.'

'That's very natural.'

'But suppose he breaks into my flat?'

'Do you have an alarm system?'

'Yes.'

'And all doors and windows have a good locking system?'

'I think so, but I don't really know anything about such things.'

'I'll get the home security officer to call round and check everything out for you.'

'When?'

'I'm not certain if he's on duty today. But he'll be with you tomorrow morning.'

'Can't you come along and advise me right away?'

Gloria had taught him that a person's reactions to events were always subjective, not objective. The odds against anyone breaking into Genevieve's flat to rape her, following the telephone call, might logically be a thousand to one, but for her they were evens or perhaps odds on. 'Tell you what. I'll nip in as soon as I can and give everything the once-over so that you'll feel safe tonight.'

'I'm most terribly grateful.'

After he'd rung off, he went along to Wyatt's room. 'Sarge, I've just had Miss Varney on the blower. She's very worried.'

'What is it this time – a curious window cleaner?'

'She's had another dirty telephone call.'

Wyatt leaned back in his chair, belched quietly. 'Didn't you tell me the case was as good as wrapped up even if we couldn't charge Wolf because Steve had made him so shit-scared he wouldn't dare even to talk about buttered crumpets over the phone?'

'That's right.'

'Now you're telling me that that's wrong.'

'Maybe, maybe not. She's not certain it's the same man.'

'The men are queuing up for full-frontal chats?'

'It sounds unlikely, but the real point is, she's scared that whoever he is, he'll break into her flat and rape her. I tried to say how unlikely that was, but she wasn't having it. So I said I'd get George to check the security out tomorrow. She didn't like the idea of waiting and so I promised to give the place the once-over myself. It'll add to the PR image and maybe I'll be able to find out if it was just Wolf trying to disguise his voice. The problem is, that'll leave CID bare.'

Wyatt rubbed his chin. 'I'll be around for a good while yet.'

'Then I'll nip across to see her and sniff out what I can.'

'Just watch where you put your nose when you're sniffing.'

* * *

Genevieve opened the door of the flat. 'It's so kind of you to come here.'

He stepped inside. 'It's the least I can do.' Her blouse enjoyed considerable décolletage and her skirt was short and full. He found himself wondering how much he'd see if he bent down to pick up something from the floor.

She led the way into the sitting room. 'I hope you don't mind?'

'What exactly won't I mind?'

'When I'm worried, I drink champagne because the bubbles help to make things right. But I don't like drinking on my own, so I put a bottle in the fridge for when you called. You will have a drink with me, won't you?'

He smiled. 'Provided I don't return to the station singing, "The policeman's lot is a happy one," it should be safe.'

'That's great.'

He watched her leave. She made him think of open moors on sunny days; but open moors with private little hollows observed only by the birds and the bees.

She returned with a salver on which were an ice bucket with a bottle in it and two flutes. She set the salver down on an occasional table.

He and Gloria had cracked a bottle of champagne on her birthday, a week before she had said that she thought she was pregnant once more. If they could have foretold the future, they'd not have drunk so cheerfully . . .

'You're looking sad.'

'Sorry.'

'Something's wrong?'

'Looking at the champagne made me remember the last time I drank some.'

'And that wasn't a happy occasion?'

'It was very happy because it was my wife's birthday. But not long after, she discovered she was pregnant and . . .'

'She'll be all right. Sometimes I'm psychic, and I know she will.' She struggled with the wire cage enclosing the cork. 'Damnit, I can never manage these things. Would you?'

He stood and crossed the room. As she passed him the bottle, their fingers briefly touched. Silk, he thought. He eased the wire loose, revolved the bottle about the cork to free it, poured out two glassfuls.

'Not a drop lost! You're obviously someone who does everything perfectly,' she said as she took a glass from him. She crossed to one of the armchairs and sat.

He was annoyed to discover that he had instinctively watched to see how far up her thighs her dress rode as she sat.

'I really am grateful for your coming here. I've been so scared.'

'You needn't be. As I've told you, the kind of man who makes obscene calls is almost always far too timid to do anything which might put him in the slightest physical danger.'

'I know, but I still . . . I'm being very stupid, aren't I?'

'Far from it.'

'But when he talked about rape being so much more satisfying . . .'

He was about to ask her if she'd activated the alert alarm when he remembered that he'd been so certain the trouble was sorted out that he'd advised the telephone company to remove the equipment. 'Have you thought any more about whether it was the same man?'

'I've thought a lot. And I can't be certain, but I think it was and he was trying to disguise his voice and that's why I started thinking it was him. Is that possible?'

'Very much so. But just to try to sort things out, concentrate on the general cadence of the two voices and tell me if they seem to have been the same.'

After a moment, she said: 'I think they were.'

'Did he talk about the same things and describe them in the same terms?'

'He never said before how satisfying rape was, but the way he described rape was similar.'

Despite her answers, he still found it difficult to accept that a man like Wolf would have ignored the warning he had received. 'I'll have another word with the man and make quite certain that if it was him this last time, he doesn't carry on.'

'It's wonderful having someone like you to look after me.'

The way in which she said that made him feel ten feet tall.

She stood, picked out the bottle from the ice bucket, crossed and refilled his glass. Because of the depth of her neckline, as she poured he was able to see the curves of her breasts, unhindered by any brassière. He jerked his gaze away.

She refilled her own glass, sat.

'As soon as I've finished my drink, Miss Varney, I'll . . .'

'For heaven's sake, Miss Varney makes it sound as if you regard me with the deepest suspicion. Genevieve.'

'When I've finished my drink, I'll check out the flat's security.'

'Why are you always in a rush?'

'Because, unfortunately, I'm always on duty.'

'Couldn't you say that a near-hysterical woman refused to let you leave in a hurry?'

'My sergeant wouldn't believe me.'

'I could always add a scratch or two for colour.'

He hoped his laugh sounded carefree.

She went into her bedroom and changed into sweater and jeans. Back in the sitting room, she played a Louis Armstrong disc. Trent had wanted her to make a move right away. She had counselled patience. Deny a horse its oats and it became hungry; deny a man, and he became frantic.

Wolf was lupine in name only. Plump, slackly muscled, his normal expression one of weak worry, Sheep would have been more fitting. 'I swear to God it weren't me.'

'She says it was the same caller as before,' replied Carr. 'That makes it you.'

'I ain't never made that kind of a call. What's more, I couldn't of phoned her this morning.'

'Why not?'

'I was in church.'

'Like I was having breakfast with Madonna.'

'Ask my ma.' Wolf's fingers plucked the air as he stood near the small boarded-up fireplace, on the mantelpiece of which were several grunge holiday mementoes.

'Mothers don't make reliable witnesses because they can get so sentimental they tell fibs about sons even like you.'

'Then ask the vicar. I'm a sidesman.'

It was too unlikely a scenario to be disbelieved. Which meant that, despite the odds, it had been a second man who'd phoned Genevieve that morning. And, contrary to what he'd said more than once, he might well pose a physical threat.

He left a few minutes later, pursued by frantic calls that Wolf had been telling the truth, the whole truth, so help him God, the twelve apostles, and serried ranks of archangels.

It was quicker to go along the back streets, even though the traffic in the centre of the town was likely to be considerably lighter than on a week day. Egremont Road proved to be solid with parked cars and he had to leave his one road away.

He climbed the steps of number 36 and pressed the flat 3 button on the entryphone. There was no response. The previous visit but one, she'd been having a shower. As he pressed the button a second time, he lathered her back . . .

He turned, descended the steps, and began to walk to his car. He wished he did not have so active an imagination. He concentrated on remembering to get on to BT to ask them to replace the Caller Display and the alert units.

12

Carr went along to Wyatt's room once again and finally found the detective sergeant there. 'I've found out where Mrs Simpson's living.'

'From the time it's taken, she's probably died from old age.'

'I'll go and get a statement from her. And since she's not far from Miss Varney, I thought I'd call on her and tell her the telephone people will be along soon to reinstal the units.'

Wyatt, who'd been standing by the side of the desk, crossed to the window and looked out. 'You're sure it wasn't Wolf again?'

'I had a quick word with the vicar and he says that obviously he can't vouch for every moment, but he reckons Wolf must have been there throughout.'

'It's one hell of a coincidence.'

'But if it wasn't Wolf, it's happened.'

He turned round. 'Have you fixed for George to check the flat's security?'

'I had a look round yesterday and reckon it's about as good as it can be without spending a fortune. The main thing is, there's a panic button and the line goes direct through to control. Provided she doesn't open the door to anyone she doesn't know, she should be safe.'

'Still get George there.'

'OK.'

'How's Gloria?'

70

'She was in one of her down moods last night.'

'Sorry to hear that . . . Freda said she'd be popping in this morning. Might help to cheer her up.' He crossed to the chair behind the desk, sat. 'You can get moving – the work's piling up and Jerry's called in sick.'

'What's up with him?'

'Flu. Says he's in bed. When I started in the force, a dose of flu wasn't a good enough excuse for turning up five minutes late.'

'Things have changed since Robert Peel.'

'Bloody funny.'

Carr drove in the CID Escort the seven miles to Blenchthorne, once a small village serving a local community, now several times that size and largely populated by commuters who had little relationship with the countryside.

Mrs Simpson was staying with her mother, who had been ill, in one of the small council bungalows for elderly people. Her mother had recovered sufficiently to be garrulous and querulous, and it took him over three-quarters of an hour to obtain the witness statement.

He returned to the Escort. Did he sneak a very quick visit to the hospital? Since he'd been held up for so long, time had become at a premium and it surely was an idea he had to forget. He started the engine. He'd been very quick to come to that decision. Because his visit to the hospital the previous evening had been so painful, with Gloria in tears? A sense of guilt dictated that he would visit her. Provided only that if Genevieve were at home, he could get away from her flat after no more than a couple of minutes.

She was at home. She was wearing a print frock that moulded her body with subtlety. 'Come on into the other room.'

'I can't stay . . .'

'You're not rushing off before you've arrived.' She tucked her arm around his. 'Not after I've spent so long

71

hoping against hope that you'd come.' She moved slightly so that his arm was more firmly against her body. 'I don't suppose you've any idea of how a pair of broad shoulders restores courage.'

Even through the sleeve of his jacket he could feel – or his imagination assured him he could feel – the swell of her breast. He said hurriedly: 'I've just dropped by to tell you an engineer will be along some time today to reinstal the alert unit.'

'That's all?'

'As I had a look at security arrangements yesterday, there's no point in my checking them again. The home security officer will be . . .'

'That's all?'

'What are you getting at?'

'It didn't cross your mind that it would be nice to see me again?'

'I . . .' He stopped.

'You?' she said mockingly.

'I'm here on duty.'

'Which precludes any thought of pleasure? There, I've embarrassed you.'

'No,' he said stiffly.

'You mustn't be thought to be paying a compliment to a lady or she might get the wrong impression? I'm not going to admit what kind of impression I have of you or you'll become very bigheaded.'

'I must move on.' He tried to free his arm.

'I'm sorry, but you mustn't.' She pulled his arm more tightly into herself. 'You're not leaving until you hear what's happened.'

'Another phone call?'

'Are you suddenly in less of a rush?'

'Have you had another obscene telephone call?'

'Shall we go through?' She uncoupled her arm, crossed the hall and went into the sitting room.

He hesitated, then followed her, unable to prevent himself wondering if under her flirtatious manner there was a warmer, more sincere emotion.

'Champagne?'

'Nothing, thanks.'

'Has anyone ever told you that sometimes you can be an absolute bore?'

'Virtually everyone.'

'Then it's time you proved virtually everyone is wrong.' She turned and left the room.

He'd given her the message that was the reason for this visit and so, convinced that her reference to some further development was a lie, there was nothing to prevent his leaving and every reason for his going. He stayed.

She returned and put the salver down. 'Will you be butler?'

'I said I didn't want anything.'

'Butlers buttle and then stand and watch.'

He opened the bottle of Veuve Clicquot and filled one glass. He hesitated, heard her chuckle, filled the second one.

She wound her arm around his, held the glass to her lips. 'Whom do we drink to?' Her deep blue eyes gazed directly into his, her lips were slightly parted.

'Peace and goodwill to all mankind.'

'And what do you wish all womankind?'

'That's your toast.'

'Then I'm going to be really selfish. Never mind the rest of womankind, let's drink to us.'

He pulled his arm free, slopping a little champagne as he did so. 'Have you received another obscene telephone call?'

'No.'

'Then what's happened? If anything has.'

'Don't you ever relax?'

'When I'm working, I work.'

'How committed! How commendable! How bloody boring!' She crossed to the settee, sat. She patted the cushion by her side. 'Come and show me what you're like when you're just a teeny weeny little bit less committed.'

He sat on one of the armchairs.

'So I have to set the scene?' She picked up a large brown envelope with her left hand, stood, crossed to sit on the arm of his chair. Her left breast rested against his cheek. He shifted until his head was clear.

'Are you comfortable?' she asked ironically.

He didn't answer.

She emptied her glass, reached across him to put it down on the table on the far side of his chair. For several seconds, he could feel her soft warmth. This time, he did not move.

'I'm not certain whether to show you.'

'Show me what?'

'Mine, if you'll show me yours.'

'Show me what?'

'What came in the post this morning. The problem is, you get embarrassed so easily.'

'What was in the post?'

'It won't upset you?'

'How the devil do I know until you tell me what it was?'

'A touch of temper?'

'Look, if you're not going to tell me . . .'

'But I am. After you've refilled our glasses.'

'Did that envelope in your hand come in the post this morning?'

'How very clever of you to deduce that.'

'Cut it out, will you. What's in it?'

'I said, I'll show you when there are more bubbles in our glasses.'

He refilled their glasses, remained standing. 'What's in it?'

She sipped champagne. 'I'm not going to show you anything all the time you stand there looking like a boy bear that's been climbing over barbed wire and slipped.'

He sat and she snuggled up against him. She dropped the envelope on to his lap.

One end had been slit with a knife and he drew out several glossy six-by-eight photographs. They could not have been more explicit and for once the performers looked as if they were enjoying themselves. The leash about his self-control slipped.

'Do you think that couple are double-jointed?' she asked, indicating the most athletic of the performers. She slid off the arm of the chair on to his lap. 'Wouldn't you think that something simpler would be more fun as one wouldn't have to concentrate so hard on not breaking anything?' She nibbled his lip. 'Are you a missionary or a cannibal?' She kissed him and her tongue slid between his lips and began to dance a samba . . .

She stepped out of the shower and began to dry. Poor bastard! He'd looked like a St Bernard in mourning as he'd left.

13

Carr entered the CID general room. Atkin, as usual, speaking before thinking, said: 'My God, you look like a man who's had a night to forget!'

'Shut up,' said Buckley roughly.

Belatedly, Atkin recognized his faux pas. 'I only . . .' He trailed off into silence.

Carr sat at his desk. The previous day, he'd not returned to the station after leaving the flat, but had phoned in to report that he'd suddenly been taken ill. The previous evening, and seemingly for much of the night, he'd suffered mental hell. And what had added further self-contempt had been the fact that one small part of his mind had been remembering, not with contempt, no, but with awed boasting, the breaches of those few barriers which Gloria had always asked him to observe.

The internal phone on Buckley's desk buzzed. He lifted the receiver, listened, called across to Carr. 'The skipper wants a word in his room.'

Wyatt was wearing a polo-neck sweater that looked as if it had been knitted by someone who'd been given the wrong measurements. 'How are you feeling today?'

'Not so bad.'

'Are you sure you should have come in?'

'It's probably only a touch of the flu and like you said, that's no excuse for being off duty.'

'That was the old days when sergeants had to take the rough with the smooth. If I catch it, I'll have words

76

with you ... I imagine you didn't visit Gloria last night?'

That's right, push the knife in deeper, Carr thought bitterly. 'I managed to find Mrs Simpson and get her statement. Don't suppose it will help.'

'That's Cumbria's worry, not ours. Did you get as far as the Varney woman?'

'Yes.'

'I still have trouble in believing it wasn't Wolf making that last call. It's asking for one hell of a coincidence for one heavy breather to tune in just as the previous one has closed down.'

'According to the vicar ...'

'I read your report. But if he was doing his job properly, he'd have been concentrating on the unseen, not the seen.'

'Whatever, right now I reckon we have to accept that Wolf didn't make that call ... There's something more. When I saw Miss Varney, she showed me what had arrived in the morning post. Eight porno photos.'

Wyatt sat back in the chair. 'I'm beginning not to like the sound of things. Any accompanying comments?'

'Nothing.'

'Where was the letter posted?'

'I ...' Carr became silent.

'You're not saying you never checked? Let's have the envelope and find out.'

'I ... I forgot to get it from her.'

'I just don't believe this!'

'Sarge, the flu was making me feel lousy.'

'Addling your brains, more like. Strewth, if the Old Man ever gets to hear about this, your nuts will be in the grinder. Were the photos rough action?'

'Couldn't have been rougher.'

'So she was shocked and disgusted?'

'I suppose so, but by the time I arrived she must have got used to them.'

77

'You're making it sound like you and her don't share vibes . . . You'd best collect the photos and envelope and ask her for a set of prints for comparison.' He reached across the desk to pull across four folders, read the identifying labels and selected one. 'House in Felstone. Alarm goes on the blink, owners gets in touch with the company which installed it and does the servicing, robbery that night. That's the third job with the same pattern, so even a D C with addled brains ought to be able to work out where to start looking.'

The telephone on the wall of the canteen rang and a P C at the nearest table answered it. 'D C Carr!' he called out.

Carr stood and crossed to the phone.

'Love, it's Gloria. I've been lucky and managed to borrow a mobile, so I don't have to try and get someone to plug in a phone for me . . . Is something the matter?'

Had woman's intuition led her to guess the truth? 'Why should anything be?' he asked, his voice suddenly hoarse.

'You didn't come to see me last night. I'm sorry to fuss like this, but I've been worrying.'

'I wasn't feeling too fit and as there's been a lot of flu around, I reckoned I might have caught it and ought to stay away from you.'

'But if you've got flu, you shouldn't be working, you ought to be home, in bed.'

'When I woke up this morning I didn't feel any worse, so I decided it couldn't be flu. And we're short-handed with people off sick and away on courses.'

'When will you have the sense to put yourself before the work?'

'There's no call to worry.'

'I do worry . . . You don't sound right.'

'I'll survive.'

'I'm telling you, you'd better!'

'How are things with you?'

78

'One of the specialists stopped by for a chat. He said that if everything goes along as it is now, I don't have to worry. I wish . . .'

'You wish what?'

'That he didn't try to jolly me along so. It makes me think that either he reckons I'm a fool, or he's lying.'

'It's a tradition with doctors to think women fools. It bolsters their egos.'

'I know I shouldn't keep becoming so terribly de-pressed, but I can't help it. I promise you, I really can't.'

'D'you think I don't know that?'

'But it's so unlike me. The trouble is, it's so difficult to forget what's happened before.'

Was memory the greatest cross a man had to bear?

'Are you still there?'

'Of course I am.'

'Fed up with my moaning?'

'Just wishing I could do something to help.'

'What do you think that talking to you now is doing? It's like suddenly seeing sunshine . . . The woman on the switchboard said she thought you were in the canteen and it sounds that that's right. What's for lunch?'

'Shepherd's pie or beef stew. I chose the pie because sometimes it's edible.'

'Poor darling. Missing home cooking?'

'Almost as much as you.' One could be a hypocrite even when telling the truth.

'When I'm home, I'll do a chicken Kiev.'

'Followed by a chocolate mousse?'

'It's a promise . . . I must ring off now because it's so expensive over a mobile and the man who lent it to me won't let me pay. If you're not feeling up to it, for good-ness sake don't bother to come here tonight.'

'I'll be along.'

'Goodbye, my darling.'

He replaced the receiver on its wall mounting.

*　*　*

He was cooking breakfast on Wednesday morning when he heard the postman push the mail through the front-door flap. He spooned fat over the two fried eggs to solidify their tops, used a fish slice to transfer them on to two slices of buttered toast, turned off the gas under the coffee machine which was hissing, set the plate on the kitchen table, poured out a mug of coffee. He then went through to the hall and picked up the four letters which lay on the floor.

Back in the kitchen, he sat on the stool, ground salt and pepper on to the eggs, speared the first of these with the knife so that the yolk ran out over the toast. As he ate, he added milk and two spoonfuls of sugar to the coffee. He checked the mail. A letter to Gloria from Swansea – her great aunt; closing on ninety but still able to write a firm hand – and a second one which he thought was from her friend who dated back to their schooldays. A brown envelope with a second-class stamp was almost certainly a bill and was best left unopened for the moment. Finally, a large plain envelope with his name and address in awkward capitals, as if written by a child. He opened it. Inside was a single photograph. Initially, he accepted that this was of a highly pornographic nature, but it took him a couple of seconds to recognize that the man, face grimacing with passion, was he.

Shock brought the outside world to a halt. It gripped him tightly enough to squeeze his lungs. It caused his mind silently to shout a panicky denial.

The world resumed. He turned the photo over; there was no writing on the back. He ballooned the envelope; there was nothing left inside.

He pressed the button of flat 3 for the fourth time. For the fourth time, there was no response.

The front door opened and a woman stepped out; middle aged, dressed for comfort and not smartness. She went to shut the door.

'Hang on,' he said.

'I beg your pardon?'

'Leave the door, will you? I need to go in.'

'I'm not certain . . .'

'Detective Constable Carr.' He showed her his warrant card.

'I'm sorry, I didn't realize.' Then she said curiously: 'Is something wrong?'

'It's just that I need a word with Miss Varney because she's been having a spot of trouble.'

'I heard about that. It's all rather disturbing. I mean, this isn't that kind of a neighbourhood.'

He was in far too much of a hurry to stand and discuss the neighbourhoods in which obscene telephone calls might reasonably be expected. 'I'm sure it isn't. Thanks.' He moved past her and went inside.

He climbed the stairs, knocked on the door of the flat; knocked again when nothing happened. Knocked a third time just to make certain. Then he began work. In the course of their careers, most detectives learned something about picking locks, especially if they'd had contact with the old-style housebreakers who preferred skill to a sledgehammer and a sawn-off twelve-bore. If on leaving she had secured all the locks fitted to the front door, he accepted that he would be unable to break in, but many people carelessly secured only the most accessible and easily worked lock. He brought a small bunch of picks, which resembled dentist's probes, from his pocket and used them in turn to try to force the main lock halfway up the leading edge of the door. The fourth one moved the tumblers. He turned the handle and pushed and the door opened.

The flat had been cleared of all personal possessions and nothing remained to give the slightest hint as to where she might have gone. In the smaller bedroom, a hole had been bored through the wall – virtually invisible in the larger bedroom because of the patterned wallpaper. When he looked through this, he had a clear view of the bed – the view the camera had had.

The practised skill with which she had seduced him – and in the circumstances this reversal of normal practice was not the farcical suggestion it might seem – the techniques she had used to lift him into fields of passion he'd only previously reached in his imagination, and her readiness to play her part in compromising him, marked her as a Tom despite her air of innocence which had so fooled him. Why? Blackmail? But any intending blackmailer would have to be a fool to presume he enjoyed even the shadow of wealth as a mere detective constable, or that he could alter the course of an investigation. And whoever had set this up clearly was no fool.

14

When Carr drove into the courtyard, Wyatt was by the far line of cars. The detective sergeant hurried across to where he parked.

'I've been shouting for you all morning.'

Since it was only a quarter to ten, that was a gross exaggeration. But Carr contented himself with saying: 'Sorry, Skipper. I went straight from home to Miss Varney's flat to ask for the photos and the envelope they were in.'

'What stopped you doing that yesterday?'

'She was out.'

'You should have phoned in first thing this morning to say what you were doing. You know the rules.' Wyatt's regard for the sanctity of rules was often the cause of amusement or resentment. 'Let's have them, then.'

'She wasn't at home.'

'And it's taken you the best part of two hours to discover that?' Wyatt ostentatiously sighed. 'Look, Mike, I know you're not going to miss the chance to slip in and see Gloria, but for Pete's sake, keep things reasonable. I had the Old Man asking for you and had to cover.'

'Thanks.'

'Just remember that my good nature's not elastic . . . The engineer from Malicious Calls has been on the blower to say he's tried to get hold of the Varney woman to arrange a time for the reinstallation of the equipment, but can't get any answer. And you've found her out each time. We know the phone calls shocked and frightened her, so d'you think it's possible the photos were the last straw and she's panicked and cleared off?'

'It's possible.'

'What's her job?'

'She never said.'

'Living in Egremont Road, it's either got to be a good one or she has a nicely rich daddy. What about relatives or a boyfriend?'

'She never mentioned anyone.'

'Seems you didn't chat her up at all?'

'I'm a married man.'

'Sounds good. But then maybe the temptation wasn't all that strong . . . Until we can contact her again, there's nothing more we can do. So get your nose hard down on all the work you ought to have cleared up days ago.'

There was little more depressing than an empty house. Carr threw his mackintosh over the chair in the hall, went through to the larder and poured himself out a heavy gin and tonic. Then, wanting the sound of voices, he moved into the sitting room and switched on the television. *Coronation Street*. He switched the set off, not bothering to channel hop. *Coronation Street* was one of Gloria's favourite programmes.

He drank. If only he had been leading a normal married life, he would not have become so sexually intrigued; if only he had not been so sexually intrigued, he would never have slid into becoming so sexually attracted that he lost all self-control. If only. The two most futile words in the language.

The phone rang. Because he so needed to be taken out of himself, he immediately decided this was someone ringing to invite him out to supper. Both Jean and Allison had promised to do so, yet so far had not. Jean's husband was a bore, Allison's children were a menace; in his present mood, he was prepared to find either husband or

84

children acceptable company. Carrying the glass into the hall, he lifted the receiver. 'Mike speaking.'

'How did you like the photograph?'

He focused his mind, knowing that he was going to have to fight long and hard. 'It's extraordinary what can be done with computers these days.'

The caller laughed. The line went dead.

He was bewildered. If this was an attempt to blackmail, why hadn't any demand been made? If it wasn't blackmail, what the hell was it? A practical joke? What joker would go to such elaborate lengths and expense – Genevieve's services would have cost big money?

He was duty bound to report the matter to the DI because it might, despite the doubts just raised, be an attempt to blackmail him into perverting the course of justice. But to look at things from a practical point of view, at the moment he could tell the DI nothing that would help identify either the caller or his motive. Better to wait until there was something definite before he suffered the humiliation of having to admit that he had screwed a Tom while his wife was in hospital, desperately trying to keep their baby alive.

Conscience was strange. On Tuesday and Wednesday it had tortured him, today it lay quiescent, yet the facts hadn't changed. Was it self-defence or cowardice which made him remember policemen he'd known who'd had nibbles on the side; the inspector who had run his hand over every new WPC's bottom to gauge the strength of her desire for promotion; the car teams who traditionally were offered quick freebies for ignoring kerb crawlers? The marriages of most of them had survived. It was the knowledge, not the act, which destroyed marriages.

He parked in front of the hospital, picked up the carrier bag from the front passenger seat, locked the car, walked past the east wing and along to the main entrance.

When Gloria saw him, she managed a smile. That was a

good sign. He bent down and kissed her, handed her the carrier bag, nodded a hullo at the woman in the next bed, sat on the edge of Gloria's bed.

She opened the carrier bag and examined the contents of the small bags inside. 'You must have bought the whole shop.'

'After choosing the pears, apples, and peaches, the chap who was serving me said the grapes were special.'

She brought out one of the small bags, reached inside to pull off a large green grape from the stalk, ate it. 'That's right, it's absolutely delicious. You're so clever!'

'Who am I to disagree, even if I don't think I can honestly claim much credit in this case.'

'It's wonderful seeing you so much more cheerful.'

Could that have been a more ironic remark?

'I was getting worried at seeing you look so down.'

'It was the flu that turned out not to be flu.'

'It was you working too hard. The next time I see Mr Hoskin, I'm going to give him an earful.'

'Just wait until after the promotion lists have come out, will you? Right now, he's edgy.'

'Suppose he does go to HQ, who do you think will take over E division?'

'I've no idea beyond the fact that it won't be Sean.'

'That won't worry him. The last time Freda came, she said he can't wait to retire.'

'Which is hardly surprising. He spends most of his time harking back to the days when the bobbies patrolled the streets on foot and the public looked on them as friends. It's never going to be like that again.'

'More's the pity.'

'You can't turn the clock back.'

'But why do things always have to change for the worst? Nowadays, it's sleaze and brutality.'

'It's not as bad as the media make out. And in any case, the pendulum will soon swing back and we'll all be putting frilly lace around piano legs.'

'I don't believe that ever really happened. It's a myth that's used to deride Victorian values.'

'When one reads about the conditions so many people lived under in those days, the values need deriding.'

She reached across and put her hand on his. 'Do you know one of the things I most like about you?'

'My handsome profile?'

'The way you really care about other people; the fact that you'd never knowingly hurt anyone . . . And that's true, so don't get all embarrassed.'

It hadn't been embarrassment, it had been the return of a sharpened conscience. He hurriedly changed the conversation. 'Can I have just one grape to taste what they're like?'

'For heaven's sake, have as many as you can eat.'

He picked a couple off the stalk. 'They are good! I'll get some more.'

'Not for a day or two, not with all the other fruit you've brought. Which reminds me – though I can't think why it should – who sent the letter?'

'What letter?'

'The one that came this morning.' She pointed at the bedside table.

He saw a large white envelope on which her name and the hospital's address were written in childish capitals.

'Well?'

'How am I supposed to be able to answer without knowing what's inside?'

'But that's the whole point. All that's inside is a photo of you.'

With a sense of shock, he realized why the writing had seemed familiar. Whoever had addressed that envelope was the same person who had addressed the envelope he'd received the previous day.

She chatted on. 'At first I thought you must have sent it and someone else had addressed the envelope . . .' She stopped. Her voice rose and sharpened. 'What's wrong. Mike, are you ill?'

The woman in the next bed leaned across. 'Shall I ring for the nurse, dear? I remember when my Bill had his stroke. Talking to me, just like you and your hubby, and all of a sudden, he went all limp . . .'

Ironically, it was the lengthy and unwelcome description of a medical disaster that enabled him to pull his thoughts together. The photograph in the envelope could not be similar to the one he had earlier received or Gloria would have been frantic, probably hysterical. 'Sorry about that,' he said. 'A touch of wind. There was steak and onions for lunch and I had a double helping of onions.'

'In which case, I haven't got much sympathy for you; you know what too many onions do to you . . . Now, who sent the photo?'

He picked up the envelope and brought out the photograph. Of snapshot size, it showed him about to enter their front garden; his right hand was on the gate, in his left were two plastic bags, one obviously heavier than the other; the collar of his mackintosh was turned up . . . The last time he'd gone shopping, he'd bought one frozen meal and an apple pie at Marks & Spencer's, and sugar, milk, bread, and jam at Sainsbury's; the wind had been rising and sufficiently biting to remind people that it was nearing the middle of winter. 'I don't know anything about it.'

'But you must.'

'I can only suppose one of the lads took it for a lark.'

'Why on earth should he do that?'

'To show you what a good housewife I've become, doing the shopping.'

'That's daft.'

'You know what they can be like when they're off duty. Mad. Like three days ago. Elmo put a sticker on the back of Hugh's mac just as he was leaving the station and the poor devil didn't know anything about it until he reached home and his wife saw it. Know what it said? "I refuse to come out".'

'You're having me on.'

'Straight.'

'But Hugh, of all people!' She giggled.

He returned the photograph to the envelope, slipped that into his coat pocket. He was thankful that she had not stopped to wonder how one of the other DCs could have known when he would be shopping.

A quarter of an hour later, he returned to his car. He sat behind the wheel, stared through the windscreen at the shifting pattern formed as a streetlight shone through the leafless branches of an oak tree that were moving to the wind. One or more men had waited in a parked vehicle to photograph him. They had him targeted . . .

He'd promised himself he'd talk to the DI the moment he had anything definite to report. It had been a decision that had allowed him to regain a measure of self-respect – however weak he might have been, in the future he would have the strength to do his duty despite the accompanying humiliation.

There was no fool like an optimistic fool. The second photograph might have been sent to Gloria, but the message was for him. Either he cooperated fully – which meant secretly – or she would receive another photograph and this would be a companion to the one they'd sent him.

He was in bed, trying to read but unable to concentrate, when the phone rang. His immediate thought was that Gloria had been taken suddenly and dangerously ill. He flung back the bedclothes and raced downstairs. 'Yes?' he said hoarsely, when the receiver was still some way from his mouth.

'Did your wife like the photo of you?'

For a second, he knew both relief and fear; relief that this did not concern Gloria directly, fear because he was about to be drawn further into the nightmare. 'Leave her out of this.'

'But she's an interested party, isn't she? Still, maybe there'll never be any need to find that out.'

'What do you want?'

'Cooperation.'

'Doing what?'

'Finding out if anyone's been fingered for the raid in West Street, Parkinham Bay.' The line went dead.

He gripped the receiver so tightly he might have had his hands around the blackmailer's throat.

15

After hours of mentally struggling to escape the inescapable, he finally accepted that he had either to betray himself or accept that Gloria would learn he had betrayed her. Since he dare not face the consequences of the latter, he had to accept those of the former. Logically, therefore, he could do nothing but await events. Yet he was a fighter and even if the outcome of the fight were predetermined, he'd go on fighting . . .

He waited until he was the only person present in the general room, dialled F division and asked to speak to the duty DC. By lucky chance, this proved to be a man with whom he'd been at training college and for a while their conversation was personal. Then he said: 'Can you say if anyone's been kitted out for the raid in West Street, Parkinham Bay?'

'We've no names as yet. All we can be certain of is that they were a bunch of rank amateurs.'

'What?' This was totally unexpected.

'Tried to break into the store through the stoutest door; when that failed, they smashed through a window which set the alarms off and made 'em run; crashed the getaway car. The Keystone Crooks . . . Have you turned up something that'll give us a lead?'

'Nothing definite, just a faint whisper. But that said that they were a smart mob.'

'Then you can tell your faint whisperer he's full of bull.'

'I'll do that.'

'Now we've made contact, let's have a few jars together one evening?'

'Great idea. But it'll have to wait. Gloria, my wife, is in hospital, so I can't really get away.'

'That's tough. Nothing serious, I hope?'

'Pregnancy problems.'

'Aren't there always? Jane had a hell of a rough time . . .'

After ringing off, Carr tried to answer the question that that phone call had posed. Why was a man cunning enough to set up the blackmail interested in a bunch of incompetents? Because they weren't the amateurs F division judged them to be and it had been a run of bad luck which they'd suffered? Because one of them was a close relative who stupidly imagined himself to be equally smart? . . . Surely the latter explanation was much more likely to be the correct one? The jealous sibling was as common in the criminal world as in the honest one. Accept this and then his betrayal of his job and his honour could be of relatively little consequence. Some of the weight was lifted off his mind.

He phoned BT's Malicious Calls bureau. 'There's another problem turned up.'

'It's problems make the world turn.'

'I've been receiving calls at home from someone we need to track down. My detective inspector says to ask you to put a trace on the line.'

'No problem.'

'Is there any chance of having it installed by this evening?'

'If I make it priority. What's the best time to do the job?'

'With work the way it is here, I can't be certain when I'll be at home. The best thing is to get the key from the next-door neighbour and she's always in. My address is fifteen, Watts Road, and the spare key is with number thirteen. I'll let her know by phone to expect someone.'

'It's as good as done. One thing, though, be a pal and don't forget the requisition note, signed by the boss.'

'It'll be in the post.'

Carr replaced the receiver. He carefully did not ask himself what possible action he could take – in the unlikely event that the blackmailer were identified through any future telephone call – that would not precipitate what he was so desperate to avoid.

He parked, walked along the pavement to number 36, climbed the steps, and rang the bell of flat 2. When a woman answered him, he said: 'Detective Constable Carr, county police, Mrs Gladwin. Could I have a word with you?'

Even through the distortions of the loudspeaker she sounded worried. 'What about?'

'I'm hoping you'll be able to help me.'

The front door buzzed. He went in and climbed the stairs to the second floor. An elderly, faded woman – not the person whom he'd met on a previous visit – stood in the doorway of the flat. She asked him into the hall.

'Sorry to bother you like this.' He smiled. Gloria had once told him that he had the kind of smile which made old ladies think of their sons when young.

'That's all right. I'm not doing anything special because my husband's out and I don't have to cook his lunch. But I really don't understand how I can possibly help you.'

'I'm trying to contact Miss Varney, but she never seems to be in. I thought perhaps you'd know if she's away on holiday?'

'I'm afraid I've no idea.'

The tone as much as the words had suggested disapproval. 'You're not very friendly?'

'It's just that in the circumstances . . . I know I'm possibly being ridiculous, but . . .'

'I don't quite follow you, I'm afraid.'

'I'm not certain I should say any more.'

'I need to know,' he assured her authoritatively.

She took a deep breath. 'I never pry, but I can't help having seen some of her visitors.'

'And they are in some way unusual?'

'They are all men and except for the last time, considerably older than she. And there was the man who called at this flat, thinking it was hers. When I opened the door he looked surprised and when I told him it was the next flat up he wanted, he was terribly embarrassed as if he'd been caught doing something wrong.'

'You think she was entertaining these men?'

She showed that she did not lack a sense of humour. 'Even if she looks as if butter wouldn't melt in her mouth, I doubt all of them were uncles.'

'You made a remark that suggested the last of her visitors you saw was different?'

'There were two of them and the photographer couldn't have been more than three or four years older than she.'

'Why do you say he was a photographer?'

A quick smile. 'He had quite a lot of photographic equipment over his shoulder.'

'What day was this?'

She thought back. 'I was on my way to Maude's to go shopping and have a coffee at Leon's, so it was a Monday.'

'Last Monday?'

'That's right.'

The detective's prayer – Oh, Lord, never mind the brains, just grant me luck. 'Can you describe the two men?'

'Not really.'

'Come on, I'll bet you can. You're obviously a very observant person,' he said, shamelessly flattering her.

'But they'd already started to climb the stairs up to the top floor when I left here so all I saw of them was their backs.'

'But you know one of them was young.'

She thought about that. 'I suppose it was an impression; you know how one gains impressions without being certain why.'

94

'Of course, but that you are so sure means you must have noticed more about them than you think you did. So describe them as clearly as you can.'

The younger man had been slightly built, wearing jeans under a somewhat scruffy mackintosh; his sandals had flip-flopped as he'd moved; his mouse-coloured hair had been down almost to his shoulders and needed a good wash. His companion, perhaps in his late forties, early fifties, had presented a contrasting picture. Tall, well built, with broad shoulders; the fawn camel's-hair overcoat had fitted him with the certainty of expensive tailoring; his black, curly hair – rather like her husband's hair when he'd been young – had been carefully cut and trimmed. There was one more thing. As she'd started to go downstairs, she'd noticed a faint, attractive scent; probably an expensive aftershave lotion. 'I'm terribly sorry, but I can't help any more than that.'

'You've done twice as well as you thought you were going to,' he assured her. 'There's only one more thing and then I can leave you in peace. Would you know if Miss Varney owns or rents the flat?'

'She rents it from someone with whom we're quite friendly. Dennis Barker works in the Gulf area and when he comes back on holiday, he stays with his sister; he said it seemed ridiculous to have the flat empty for the three or four years he'd be away.'

'Does he let it direct or through an agency?'

'An agency; Imray and Philips. He reckons that they are the best in the area. We offered to help, of course, but he preferred to do everything through a professional third party in case there was any sort of trouble. To tell the truth, after that man called here by mistake, I was certain we ought to tell the agents what might be going on, but my husband wouldn't hear of it. He was afraid that to do so might end up with our being sued for slander. In this sort of situation, it's terribly difficult to know what to do.'

'Sometimes it's impossible,' he said, with more force than intended. He thanked her for her help, said goodbye, and left. As he made his way down the stairs, he thought how luck seldom ran in one direction only. Good luck had brought Mrs Gladwin out of her flat in time to see the two men, but bad luck had ensured she stepped out too late to see their faces . . . Yet she had seen the fawn overcoat and that had reminded him of the man he'd seen leaving number 36 and walking to the silver Porsche. Yet bad luck had made certain that he also had only seen the man briefly in profile and then, when near enough to make out detail, from behind. If only good luck had prompted him into noting the registration number of that Porsche. One more if only . . .

He drove around two sides of the common to join the inner ring road, turned off in time to make the one-way Bank Street, more familiarly known as the Street of Forty Thieves.

The receptionist in Imray and Philips, whose proud boast was that they'd been in business since 1876 (making them one of the original forty), phoned three partners before she found one who was free.

Evans was pleasant and helpful. After tapping out instructions on the computer keyboard, details of the letting came up on the screen; no notice of termination had been given by Miss Varney.

'When's the rent due?' Carr asked.

'At the beginning of the month.' Evans fiddled with one of his coat buttons. 'Is there some sort of trouble? Do we have to worry about the use to which the flat is being put?'

'What makes you think you have to?'

'She is a single lady and you are asking questions.'

'You think it may have been used for immoral purposes?'

'There always has to be that possibility. So difficult to prove, of course.'

96

If only that were always true.

The phone rang twice. The first time the caller was a friend, asking about Gloria; the second time, the blackmailer.

The Caller Display unit was recording blocked identification. Carr pressed down the yellow button on the alert unit.

'Well?'

'I had a word with someone in the division.'

'And?'

'It was difficult because I couldn't let him start wondering why I was so interested . . .'

'Is anyone in the bracket for the job?'

'Not at the moment.'

'Not even a whisper?'

'Not so far. But because the job was so bungled . . .'

The line was cut.

He dialled the bureau.

'Hullo, mate, I was just about to get on to you. That was from a call box in Charing Cross main-line station.'

A couple of minutes later, he went through to the larder and poured himself a gin and tonic. In the past, he'd been astonished at the way in which criminals were often so blindly optimistic. Yet he had been hoping that the man who'd planned so cleverly would make the mistake of telephoning from a private address . . .

16

Despite the invasion of the chain stores and the super-markets, Everden still boasted several small shops which specialized in quality rather than quantity. Carr walked along the pedestrianized upper High Street to the greengrocer. There were more of the large white grapes and by their side were nectarines. Asked to choose be-tween grapes and nectarines, Gloria would have hesitated. He was about to enter the shop and buy both when he remembered that after paying for lunch at the canteen, he'd had very little money left.

He walked down the High Street to his bank and inser-ted his card in the cashpoint, requested a statement. He was in credit for less than he'd hoped – only just over eighty-one pounds. There were a couple of bills which would have to be paid before the end of the month and they would swallow up a large part of that, and then there would be the continuing and unavoidable extra costs that followed from Gloria being in hospital, such as the extra petrol used in driving to and from the hospital. But he was damned if he was going to cut back on buying fruit, because it provided the only pleasure left to her. He withdrew twenty pounds.

At the greengrocer's, he bought the largest bunch of grapes on display and two pounds of nectarines. The man who served him added an extra nectarine because he had become so good a customer. He returned to the car, drove the fifteen minutes to the hospital.

As he entered the ward, the sister stopped him and called him across to the desk. 'Dr Calvin asked me to have a word with you.'

He suffered an all too familiar feeling. 'My wife's bad?'

'She has become unusually depressed and that's obviously worrying.' She spoke briskly, but not without a sense of sympathy. 'Dr Calvin wonders if there's a particular reason why she might be under additional stress?'

'None that I know of.' Then the bitter thought occurred to him that perhaps Gloria was subconsciously tuning into his emotional chaos. They had often been surprised to discover how the emotional state of one, even if carefully hidden, had affected that of the other.

'You and she haven't recently had any sort of a disagreement?'

'Of course not.' Perhaps it was the suddenly raised sense of guilt that made him say angrily: 'What d'you take me for? You really think I'd come here and have a row with her in the state she's in?'

'I'm certain you're not that kind of man, Mr Carr, but I had to ask.'

After a while, he said: 'I'm sorry.'

'Forget it . . . Dr Calvin says it's important to try to cheer her up.'

'The quickest way of doing that would be . . .' He did not finish and ignored her look of questioning curiosity.

He was shocked by Gloria's appearance. He bent down and kissed her, handed her the bag of fruit. She did not bother to examine the contents before putting it on the table.

He sat on the edge of the bed and held her hand as he chatted. For most of the time she lay still, her hand limp, her eyes unfocused. In desperation, he began to talk about the nursery, a subject that usually animated her. He said he'd seen some wallpaper that was exactly what she'd always wanted . . .

She began to cry. Then she spoke in a rush, the words

tripping into each other. The previous night, one of the other women in the ward had suffered a heart attack and had had to be rushed into intensive care; that was an omen. She was going to lose her child. He tried to make her understand how completely illogical such a belief must be, but she merely repeated herself, her voice becoming shriller. He switched the conversation, but for the rest of the visit was certain that her mind was not on what he was saying, but on her fears.

On his way out of the ward, he spoke to the sister again. 'I've done what I can. Which adds up to nothing.'

'You may have helped more than you realize, Mr Carr, just by letting her release her feelings.'

'Can't you give her something stronger to help her depression?'

'I'm afraid not, because of the baby.'

'But she can't go on as she is.'

'She may recover spontaneously. It sometimes happens that way.'

'And if it doesn't?'

'We never consider worst scenarios.' She studied him. 'It can be an equal hell for those who are nearest. If you want my advice, you'll make certain you spend the rest of the evening with friends. Worrying can't change anything.'

Good advice was given to be ignored. He returned home, repeatedly cursed the malign fate which had them in its grip, and drank too much. The nurse should have added that drinking didn't change anything either.

17

On Monday morning, the mail included a large, fibre-reinforced brown envelope, addressed in childlike capitals. It was quite some time before he overcame his reluctance to open it. Inside were three thousand pounds, in used twenty and fifty pound notes. Payment for his betrayal.

Now there could be no ifs, buts, or maybes. He should report the receipt of this money to Hoskin. He could claim he knew nothing about it, had no idea why it had been sent to him, but Hoskin would immediately suspect it was bung, even though no attempt had been made to conceal it. He'd start digging and wouldn't stop until he knew all the answers.

Carr held the thick bundle of notes between thumb and forefinger. More cash than he had ever handled before. When he passed it on, few would think him any the less of a traitor; nothing would be gained, all would be lost. So where was the logic in doing something that ended in disaster . . . ?

Four days to Christmas. Gloria had always known exactly what to give him for Christmas that would give him the greatest pleasure, while he had always had trouble thinking of a present for her. For once, that would not have been a problem if only . . . If only . . .

The nursing home was halfway up the hill, at the back of the ancient coastal town of Writstone; a large, rambling house, built for a man who had made a fortune from laxative pills when these had been considered a necessary part of every right-minded Christian's diet, it had been converted at considerable cost three years previously. It stood in grounds of just over an acre, most of which lay in front, or on the sea side, giving the impression of untrammelled space despite the surrounding housing. There was a small residential staff and a pool of part-time helpers.

Gloria's room faced south and offered a clear view of the Channel; when there was little or no haze, she could watch the passing ships through binoculars. With an imagination almost as quick and wide as her husband's, she imagined cargoes of ivory, apes, peacocks, sandalwood, cedarwood, and sweet white wine . . .

The door opened and Carr entered. 'Merry Christmas, my darling.' She smiled with a warmth not often seen.

He crossed to the bed, kissed her, handed her a small package wrapped in gift paper and tied with gold-coloured string. 'I'm afraid it's not very exciting.'

'You've already given me the most wonderful present ever. And I haven't anything for you.'

'I'll take a raincheck . . . How's junior?'

'Very active. Had two bouts of kicking this morning.'

'Then it's a he and he's in line for striker for Arsenal.' She had refused to be told the sex of the child in her womb because, he was certain, then it remained just that little fraction less of a person and so should she lose it, the loss would be that little fraction less defined.

'I wish I could get him to take his practice a little less seriously.'

They laughed. Over the past three days, they had found themselves laughing over silly little things, as they had once often done.

She untied the string, unwrapped the paper. 'Truffles! Those heavenly truffles that remind me of our honeymoon . . . You really are terrible, putting so much temptation in front of me.'

102

'You'll get added pleasure every time you give way to it.'

'You know the doctor said I still wasn't losing the weight I should.'

'Doctors are professional killjoys because that's how they make people think they're doing them some good.' He moved the chair closer to the bed, sat.

She reached out to grip his hand and squeeze it affectionately, then offered him the box. After he'd helped himself, she put a truffle in her mouth. 'They really are out of this world,' she said, as she swallowed. 'For heaven's sake, put the box out of reach or I'll eat the lot.'

He moved it to the table.

'Do you know what? I very nearly rang the building society yesterday to wish the manager as wonderful a Christmas as he's given me by letting you take out the second mortgage. He must be a very nice man.'

'He is.'

'When I'm back in circulation, I'm going to tell him face to face what it's meant to us.'

'I'm afraid you won't get the chance. He told me that he was retiring at Christmas and moving up north because that's where he's from.'

'What a pity. I'd so like to have said it.'

'I'm sure he understood when I thanked him from both of us.'

'It's wonderful to think there are still people like him around. Makes one realize that the world isn't as terrible a place as so many people try to make out.'

'Cue for heavenly choir and fade out.'

'If I weren't confined to bed, I'd hit you for that!'

He wondered what she'd do if ever she guessed the truth?

18

Because he'd had Christmas Day and Boxing Day off, Carr was on duty throughout Sunday. The day produced an average amount of crime, proving that not everyone had the holiday spirit; one hit-and-run, four driving under the influence, an attempted ram raid, a vicious mugging, four breaking and enterings, an affray leaving one of the men eyeballing death, a mare brutally injured, and an eleven-year-old girl who was missing with, as yet, no indication as to whether she had run away or been abducted. He arrived home three-quarters of an hour after he was due at the Wyatts' for supper. He quickly showered and changed into clean clothes and had opened the front door to leave when the phone rang. He hesitated. If he were delayed any further, it would make him over an hour late and that might well strain even Freda's long-suffering patience. But the caller might be Gloria who had insisted that for once he did not visit her, yet now wanted a quick word. He pushed the door shut, crossed the hall to the phone.

'It's nice to know the money's helped to move your wife into a nursing home. Warms the heart to see it do so much good.'

The mockery added extra fear. 'What do you want now?' he asked hoarsely. Belatedly, he remembered to check the Caller Display unit, then activate the alert unit.

'To hear if your wife's better with the move.'

'Leave her out of this.'

'Like I said, she's part of it.'

'I told you what you wanted to know.'

'And now I'm hoping you'll be even kinder and find out something more.'

'What?'

'Why MacClearey's employing a private army.'

'Who?'

'Even if you are a copper, you must have heard of Little Boy Blue. Makes a million quid every time he opens his mouth.'

'The pop singer?'

'There, I knew you'd be quick on the uptake.'

'What d'you mean, an army. He'll have a minder . . .'

'But since he isn't royalty on a toe-sucking expedition, why's he got half a dozen minders?' The line went dead.

He replaced the receiver. Was the blackmailer planning a job that would involve MacClearey? The pop singer was very rich and had become a noted collector of Nurnberg Faience, a fact which had become publicly known after he'd bought two incredibly expensive pieces at auction. But the blackmailer must realize that his demand for information would raise the possibility that an attempt would be made to steal part or all of his collection. Was he banking on the fact that he – Carr – would not pass on the word because to do so would mean disaster? Yet even a worm could turn and so he couldn't be certain; he had to be a man who was always certain. So was there some hidden reason for wanting the information?

The phone rang. 'Malicious Calls. That originated in a call box in Waterloo Station. Do you want exact identification of which box?'

'Thanks, but there's no point.'

He replaced the receiver. He felt frightened, bitter, uncertain, and the last thing he wanted to do was to have to be sociable, but he had no option. He dare not do anything that might raise the beginning of a question in

Wyatt's mind, and his own guilt left him scared that any unusual behaviour on his part might do that.

Freda let him into the house. 'I'm terribly sorry to be so late,' he said.

'No cause to worry, Mike. I'm an expert at slowing down the cooking when that's necessary. Go on through and have a drink with Sean and I'll get ready to dish, but first tell me, how's Gloria?'

'Last night, she was really cheerful.'

'Isn't that wonderful!'

'Almost a miracle.'

'I'm hoping to drop in and see her tomorrow morning. Presumably morning will be best since I don't suppose you can get to see her until the evenings?'

'When she was in the hospital there was often something going on nearby which meant I could sneak in during the day for a couple of minutes, but Writstone's a law-abiding place and so I have to wait until I'm off duty.'

'Then I'll make it the morning.' There was a sound from the kitchen. 'Is that the cat on the table? If it is, I'll shove it in the oven!'

He smiled at the thought, went into the sitting room. Wyatt, wearing a sweater and ancient flannels, was sprawled out in one of the armchairs, watching television. He switched off the set with the remote control. 'So you've finally made it.'

'Sorry, Skipper, couldn't get away from the factory. Seems like everyone's been busy.'

'It's all this talk about peace and goodwill. Gets the villains itchy.' He elbowed himself upright, stood. 'So what'll it be – whisky, gin, lager, sherry, or tequila?'

'Tequila doesn't sound your usual style.'

'Bill and Evelyn's present. Don't let on to Freda, but I reckon someone gave it to them and they've passed it on. You'd like some of it?'

'I'd prefer a G and T.'

'No sense of adventure? If it goes on like this, I'll put it away and hand it on next Christmas to someone else.' He crossed to a tray on which were bottles and glasses. 'Freda had a word with Gloria over the phone and says she sounds a different person.'

'She is. She's back to how she used to be and you wouldn't think she'd ever had a depression.'

'The mind's a funny thing and no mistake.' He returned and handed Carr a glass. 'There's no extra charge for sitting.' He settled, picked up the half-empty tankard from the table by his side, raised it. 'To Gloria. May her recovery be complete.'

They drank.

'Freda says you managed to raise the wind by persuading the building society to change its mind. I reckon that puts you in a class on your own!'

'I saw the manager and told him house prices might be static in some places, but they were going up around us and someone on our road had been offered five thousand more than it had been valued at a year ago; and if my place was worth an extra five thousand, that took it well clear of negative equity so surely he could lend me another three.'

'I hadn't heard that prices were rising anywhere.'

'The main thing is, he didn't argue. Maybe because I said how Gloria was getting worse all the time and I was desperate to move her to see if that would do any good. He was much more sympathetic than before. Even winked when he agreed.'

'Maybe he's human, unlike the staff at my bank . . . When you say it was a busy day, what was the score?'

Carr breathed a silent sigh of relief. Wyatt had lost all interest in how he'd been able to afford to move Gloria to the nursing home.

He'd once read that repetition dulled conscience. That seemed to be true. When he'd phoned F division to ask if they'd fingered anyone on the job in West Road, he'd felt sick. About to make a second, similar call, his only real concern was to be very careful what he said.

'Little Boy Blue?' The D C's voice was scornful. 'Can't stand the row he makes.'

'No more can I, but his name's cropped up and I'm wondering if there's anything there.'

'Hang on.'

After a couple of minutes, a second man said: 'Sergeant Grant. You're asking about MacClearey?'

'That's right, Sarge.'

'Why?'

'One of my snouts was in a pub and heard a couple of villains talking about him. I wondered if there was anything there.'

'What were they saying?'

'My snout says he couldn't get close enough to hear more than the name. Maybe he needs bunging to refresh his memory; I'm not doing that until I know it could be worthwhile.'

'Early in the month, we heard from a small-timer whose boyfriend had done the dirty on him that the mob who'd kidnapped and raped Victoria Arkwright were staking out their next victim. He couldn't identify who that was beyond the fact that the father was a mega-rich pop singer with two or more daughters ... You must remember that all forces in the country were asked to list anyone who came into that category ... Well, we narrowed the possibles down to three and one of 'em was MacClearey, who looked really promising since he's more millions than I've had hot dinners. So far, though, thank God, there's been no move against his daughters or the kids of the other two possibles.'

With a sense of sheer horror, Carr finally found the answers to the many questions he had asked himself.

'Are you still there?'

'Yes, Sarge.' His voice had become croaky.

'If your snout knows anything, bung him until he thinks his second name is Rothschild.'

'I'll do what I can, but he's not reliable.'

After the call was over, Carr crossed to the right-hand window and stared down at the slow-moving traffic. Even the police, who had to face the dark side of human nature every day, had been unable to understand how any man could be so viciously brutal as to rape a girl, subject her to further sexual torments, and deliberately infect her with the HIV virus. The men who had done that needed to be hunted down and in the regrettable absence of capital punishment, to be locked up in the toughest of prisons where the other inmates could be relied upon to make their lives hell. So he had to go to Hoskin and confess all that had happened . . .

There could only be one consequence of such action. He'd have to surrender all the remaining money which meant Gloria would have to be moved out of the nursing home and back to the hospital at the same time as she was forced to learn that her husband had been blackmailed into becoming a traitor through his adultery with a tart. One didn't need to be a doctor or a psychologist to know that her depression would return, in even deeper and more disastrous form . . . Once again, he was faced with choosing between two courses of action, neither of which he dare take . . .

He reconsidered the facts. He had no idea who the blackmailer was and had learned nothing that could identify the future victim who would replace – perhaps – the MacClearey daughters. So at this point, if he were to confess to what had happened, he would be sacrificing himself and Gloria to no practical purpose . . .

The phone rang on Tuesday night when Carr was in bed, reading. He hurried down to the hall.

'So what's the news?'

No identification of the caller's number; he pressed the alert button. 'The police warned MacClearey.'

'Why?'

The blackmailer's tones were sharper, the mockery absent; he was sweating on the answers. 'They had a whisper and told him he was one of three people whose daughters were at risk from the mob who'd kidnapped the Arkwright woman.'

'Who's the grasser?'

'It was anonymous, over the blower.'

'Did he name the mob?'

'No.'

The line went dead.

Carr found his hands were shaking. He could not begin to identify the blackmailer or do anything to prevent another brutal kidnapping. But if he were asked to give any further information that could, however remote the possibility, help to make that identification or put any girl at risk, then he would make his confession, whatever the consequences to Gloria and himself.

Malicious Calls rang to tell him that this last call had come from a call box in Cannon Street Station. The kidnapper was clearly a man of careful routine.

19

Trent walked the beach, his face dampened from the spray that was driven inshore by the wind. Who was the grasser? No one on the team; they were all solid. Yet no one outside the team could have known they were preparing to move on the MacCleareys unless he was so friendly with someone on it that confidences were exchanged . . . He mentally examined each man, searching for weaknesses, examining known friendships . . .

Nick! He came to a stop and turned to face the breaking waves. As gay as a night in Paris. Not long back, he'd been tied up with a slob called Pete Morrell. Then there'd been a row and they'd split up and Nick, as promiscuous as a barnyard rooster, had teamed up with another partner. That, so the story had gone, had left Morrell acting like he'd lost his family jewels. Nick wouldn't grass if he were offered the cast of *The Sleeping Beauty*, but he did like the booze too much and maybe sometime prior to the split he'd had a bellyful and talked, and after it, Morrell had decided to ease his hurt feelings by grassing on him . . .

Trent resumed walking. The facts fitted the possibilities, the possibilities, the facts, the more he thought about them. But to make certain, he'd have to have a chat with Morrell.

Morrell and Hamilton, his new friend, had celebrated the New Year in fitting style with the consequence that neither of them moved until the late afternoon on the

Friday. Then Hamilton, needing several hairs of the dog, went downstairs, only to find that the cupboard was bare. Cursing, he left the house and staggered along the road to the shop, run by a Pakistani family, that was open every day of the year. He bought a bottle of gin, a pack of Lucky Strike, and some chewing gum. On his return to the house, he was surprised to find that Morrell had disappeared and in the bedroom a chair had been knocked over and smashed and the mattress had been pulled off the bed. Surprise did not prevent his settling down and drinking.

They drove Morrell to an empty house in the country that was for sale. Asked if Nick had ever mentioned any details of the jobs in which he was engaged, he swore by all the saints in the calendar, and some that weren't, that Nick never, never talked business. And as for grassing to the splits . . . He'd rather have his tongue torn out than tell those bastards as much as the time. Desperation and fear had the effect, the opposite to normal, of making him sound convincing. The other two were convinced, Trent was not; he did not like to be proved wrong.

They dragged Morrell into the kitchen, tied his arms and legs together, lifted him up on to the right-hand draining board and held him so that his head was bending backwards as it hung over the sink, placing his neck under tension. Trent rammed an old cloth down his throat and poured water on this, causing him to suffer the growing agony of 'slow drowning'. They stopped before he lost consciousness and gave him time to recover, then asked him again if he'd grassed to the splits. At his denial, they resumed the treatment and repeated it until he finally signalled that he was ready to change his story. After they'd hauled him upright and removed the cloth and he had finished gagging, coughing, and the worst of his whimpering, he admitted that he had mentioned one or two things to the split who'd questioned him in the hospital after Nick had all but cut him to death. He pleaded for mercy on the grounds that he had been shocked and that he had named no names so that no real damage had been done . . .

That last so infuriated Trent that instead of spending time killing the other, he brought the length of piano wire out of his coat pocket, wound it round Morrell's throat, and pulled it tight.

The handing over of the ransom money was almost always the most dangerous time for kidnappers. Recognizing this from the beginning, Trent had carefully worked out how to eliminate all danger.

After the coming kidnapping, there would be complete silence, maintained long enough for the parents to recall every last detail of the Victoria Arkwright case and in consequence become frantic. Then they would be ordered to say nothing to the police and to advise their bank to have five million pounds ready for collection on immediate advice. The next day, they would be told to instruct their bank to transmit the money electronically to another bank in Switzerland, giving them just half an hour to comply if they wanted their daughter to remain healthy. The moment the money was transferred, the Swiss bank was to be instructed to transmit it to a bank in the Cayman Islands . . . If the police had not been kept informed, everything must be simple. If they had been, in their attempt to follow the money they would come up against the Swiss laws concerning banking secrecy which demanded proof of criminal activity before any details of an account would be released. By the time such details were provided, the money would have vanished from the Cayman bank . . .

Now that he knew that Morrell had done no more than betray facts which had enabled the police to identify MacClearey the job could continue after a replacement victim had been identified. And as to that, the gods were obviously with him. In the morning's paper had been the photograph of an attractive eighteen-year-old whose birthday party the previous night had been named the social event of the winter. Her father was mega-rich, her mother was related to the throne. Wealth and royalty, a combination made for the headlines.

It would be the heist of the century. And the more he thought of the acclaim that the job would bring him, the more convinced he became that in naming a ransom of five million, he was seriously underestimating what the market would bear.

The estate agent had little hope of selling the property to the young couple; he doubted very much that they could afford the asking price. But business was so slack that not even a distant chance could be overlooked. 'It's a big garden.'

They looked at the overgrown lawn, the weed-choked flower beds, the untrimmed hedge.

'A large garden adds considerable value. If this were neat and tidy, the price would be at least another ten thousand. There's a bargain going here.'

'Why's it been let go so?' asked the wife, wrapping the scarf more tightly around her neck to try to keep the keen easterly wind at bay.

'The owner was very old when she died and I'm afraid old people don't look after things.'

'Then the inside's in as terrible a state?'

'A little decorating and it'll be like new.' What did they expect for ninety thousand – the Taj Mahal?

'It's very isolated.'

'No more than half a mile into the village and you can see the roof of the next house through the trees.'

He led the way up the gravel path, so thick with weeds that their shoes made no sound, to the front door. He unlocked the door, waved them through.

'The hall's tiny,' she said.

114

He'd been about to ask them to move forward so that he could get far enough in to close the door, but decided not to do so and left the door ajar, despite the draught. 'I always think of a large hall as an unnecessary and wasteful luxury – you don't do anything in it but pass through, do you? Much better a slightly restricted one if that means a really generous sitting room . . . If you'll go through the first doorway, you'll see that you can have a really large party in there and you won't find yourself reaching in the next person's pocket for your handkerchief.' They did not smile. A couple of erks, he thought. 'If you would like to go through?'

She did not move. 'There's a funny smell.'

'Empty houses do sometimes have a slight scent.'

'I'd call this a stink.'

'My wife has a very keen sense of smell,' said the husband.

That was because she had such an enormous nose. 'Would you go through, please?'

They went into the sitting room. 'As you can see, it's a very light and airy room, possessing an air of gracious space. There are two radiators, with individual temperature controls, double glazing, and a TV point beyond the fireplace. The floorboards are in excellent condition and a quick coat of paint and perhaps fresh wallpaper will work a treat.'

'It is nice in here,' agreed the husband.

'It's the wrong shape,' she said.

It was always the wives, the estate agent thought; you could satisfy a starving crocodile before you could satisfy a woman.

'It's three bedrooms, isn't it?' asked the husband.

'Four, although one has to admit that the fourth one is not very large. Shall we go through and look at the dining room?'

They returned to the hall. The wife sniffed. 'It's like a dead rat.'

'There are no rats in this house, dead or alive,' the estate agent hastily assured her.

The husband liked the dining room, the wife criticized the position of the window and the single radiator.

Now quite certain that there would be no sale, the estate agent said brusquely: 'We'll have a quick look at the kitchen before going upstairs.' He led the way. 'There is a very nice cooker in place and all electrical connections for the usual washing machine, washing-up machine and . . .' He came to a stop four paces into the kitchen. There was a disgusting smell.

'Strewth!' exclaimed the husband.

'Perhaps some food has been left behind,' he said uncertainly.

'I'm not stopping in here,' the wife said. She hurried out of the kitchen, followed by her husband. The estate agent decided that in consideration of future visits with prospective clients he had to find out what was causing the stink and either remove it or, preferably, have it removed at a later date. He went round the table in the centre of the kitchen and saw a foot. He broke into a cold sweat. Even the sight of a little blood made him feel faint and the thought of a corpse . . . 'Can you come here a minute, Mr Jackson?' he called out.

The husband appeared in the doorway. 'You sound like something's up?'

'There . . . Over there . . .'

He came forward, looked to his left. 'Christ!' He ran into the hall and began to retch.

As required by law, the police doctor had declared the man dead – hardly a difficult diagnosis – photographs had been taken, a search of the house had been made, the Scene-of-Crime officer had collected up a few things which might or might not be of consequence, and now everyone was waiting for the arrival of the pathologist and the detective chief superintendent.

The detective inspector looked at his watch. 'Have you been on to the electrical company?'

'They can't do anything until tomorrow morning,' the detective sergeant replied.

'Par for the course. So what about portable lights?'

'They're on their way.'

'If the D C S ever arrives, you know what his first question's going to be, don't you? Who's the victim?'

'Show him what's left and ask him if he can recognize him.'

'I'll give you ten to one his dabs are on record.'

'A drug-related case?'

'The doc said there's no sign of drug usage.'

'Whatever, someone didn't like him.'

They heard the slam of a car door and crossed to the window of the sitting room. They saw the tall, slightly stooping figure of the detective chief superintendent approach the gate. A P C barred his way.

'Doesn't know who he is,' said the detective sergeant with pleasure.

'He'll very soon learn.'

20

If ever he'd been asked what more he wanted out of life, Wyatt would have had difficulty in answering because he was one of those few, fortunate persons who were contented with their lot. However, if pressed, he probably would have suggested that it would be nice if Evelyn's Bill was a little more considerate and if Jane could meet a respectable man who didn't wear his hair long and have earrings; what ambition he had was not for himself.

He shuffled through the papers of the opened file on the desk. The accused's arrest and his refusal to admit his obvious guilt meant there had to be two sets of witness statements, written report, fourteen forms dealing with particulars of prisoner, legal aid forms, property forms . . .

The telephone rang and a civilian telephonist said: 'There's a call from Sergeant Grant, Shropshire, for D C Carr. He's not in the general room and I wondered if you know where he is?'

'Put the call through and I'll see if I can help.' There was a sharp click. 'Wyatt here. Carr's away and not likely to be back for a while. Anything I can do?'

'It's like this. Back at the beginning of December, a small-time villain, Peter Morrell, gave us information that seemed to identify a small group of people, one of whom would be the next target of the mob who kidnapped the Arkwright girl, but he wouldn't name anyone in the mob. We narrowed the potential victims down to three and MacClearey was one of them. There's been no kidnap attempt and so we've been left uncertain whether the grass was solid or dud; uncertain until now, that is. Morrell's murder gives the answer. But since he was tortured before he was murdered, there's now another question. Why the torture? The obvious answer is that either they got wind there'd been a grass, via Morrell or the extra security precautions MacClearey took suggested this, and they had to make certain whether this was so and how serious and how detailed the grass had been. The fact that no further kidnapping attempt has been made suggests the mob has been warned off. Accept the scenario and it seems they can't have had any more information than we had. A possibility that has given our detective chief superintendent the idea that there's been a leak from our side.'

'Bloody impossible,' said Wyatt angrily. 'There's not a copper would breathe the same air as them.'

'I'll go all the way with that, but the DCS seems to be swinging more and more to the idea.'

'Then I'm glad he's your DCS and not ours . . . How can Carr possibly fit into all this?'

'He was on the blower in the middle of the month, wondering what I could tell him about MacClearey because one of his snouts had heard the name mentioned. I said to get back on to me if he learned anything definite, but there's been no buzz so I supposed he didn't. But just in case, I'd like another word with him.'

'I'll get him to ring you the moment he's back.'

Carr entered Wyatt's room. 'I've tracked down the witness and his evidence is looking good.'

'Good enough?' Wyatt asked.

'Yes, if he sticks by what he told me.'

'Let me have the report as soon as you can.'

He started to leave.

'Here, hang on a sec. Sergeant Grant from Shropshire has been on the blower and wants a word with you.

Here's the number.' Wyatt pushed across a slip of paper.

Carr picked up the paper. 'Did he say what it's about?'

'He wants to know if you've heard anything more concerning MacClearey; a small-timer who may be connected with a possible kidnapping of the MacClearey daughters has been found tortured and murdered.'

Carr felt as if he had suffered a violent, numbing blow.

Wyatt studied him. 'Are you all right? You look as if you've been reading your gravestone.'

Carr struggled to act and speak normally. 'A sudden pain in the guts, that's all. I get it from time to time.'

'You want to watch that sort of thing. Have you seen a quack?'

'He says it's only wind.'

'Then I'll thank you to get out of here before you release the pressure.'

Carr somehow managed to smile.

'How did you become interested in MacClearey?'

'One of my snouts heard a couple of newcomers mention his name.'

'In what connection?'

'My chap couldn't stay within earshot long enough to hear anything more. The name didn't say anything to me, so I phoned Shropshire to find out if it could be worth trying to learn more.'

'How d'you know to get on to them if the name didn't mean anything?'

O what a tangled web we weave, When first we practise to deceive! He struggled to give a reasonable answer. 'When I said it didn't mean anything, I meant in our job. But the name immediately made me think of Little Boy Blue, so I checked where he lived and then phoned county HQ.'

'The only thing Little Boy Blue says to me is that he blows his horn.'

'This one blows his own trumpet.'

'Don't they all ... Shropshire told you he was

connected with the Arkwright case, maybe, and to learn all you could?'

'I told my grass to keep looking and listening, but according to him the two newcomers just vanished and no one can tell him anything about 'em.'

'Get back on to him and tell him to burrow a bloody sight harder . . . The present line of thinking up there seems to be that Morrell was tortured to find out if he'd alerted our side to the fact that MacClearey was a likely target. But that thinking raises questions, like how did the mob come to suspect he might have grassed? The DCS is a right bastard because he's come up with the theory that there's been a leak from within.'

Carr experienced panic.

'Say what you like about our DCS, he'd never suggest that line. You've got to hand him that much . . . OK, get on to Sergeant Grant and tell him you can't help immediately, but you'll be putting red-hot pokers up your snout's fundament to make him try harder.'

Carr left. Wyatt scratched a tickle on his forehead, which was becoming elongated as his hair receded. He hoped that Carr's wind was not a symptom of something more serious than too much oily food – it wasn't long since that he'd read an article dealing with the social embarrassment of flatulence which had pointed out that it could be the symptom of a serious underlying complaint. He hated medical articles because they almost invariably left him suffering from whatever the article had been about. But he still read them.

It had not been the most entertaining of evenings for Wyatt. It was a rule of the house – promulgated by Freda, not him – that when visitors were present, the television was not switched on. Hearing that Jane was bringing her latest to supper, he'd started to set the video to record his favourite programme, only to discover it was no longer working. After that, it seemed only fitting that their visitor lectured them on the evils of the overconsumption of the earth's resources while eating twice as much as everyone else.

'You weren't very good company,' Freda observed, as they heard the Suzuki roar into life.

'D'you expect me to dance a jig when she brings the likes of him back?'

She smiled.

'What's so amusing?'

'You've been the same over every boy either of them has ever had in the house.'

'Because they've all been the same.'

'Some of them have been quite nice. Surely you're not saying that Bill's so awful?'

'He ought to give Evelyn more of a hand around the house now that she's preggers.'

'She's happy with the way things are.'

'That's more than I am.'

'Since it's none of your business, that doesn't matter.'

'Thanks very much.'

'Do you know what Judy said to me the other day?'

'No, but it'll have been bitchy.'

'It was easy to imagine you on the North West Frontier, loyally fighting for Queen and country without knowing why.'

'What an extraordinary thing to say.'

'She makes a point of saying odd things. But some of them have some truth in 'em.'

'You're saying you can see me chasing the fuzzy-wuzzies?'

'Only so long as they don't catch you. I read not so long ago that the women had a horrible way of killing their captives.'

He picked up the *Radio Times* and skimmed through the programmes. 'I knew it! Nothing worth watching now.'

'Then we can have a reasonably early night . . . By the way, Claude and Hetty have asked us for supper next weekend. I gave them a provisional yes. You're not on duty on the Sunday, are you?'

'I'm not down for it.'

'Then make certain you stay off. Hetty says they've given up the idea of moving.'

'I thought she reckoned that with the boys growing up so fast, they had to find somewhere with at least one more bedroom?'

'She now thinks they can manage for a couple more years and is hoping that by then the housing market will have recovered and they'll be able to get what they want for their place.'

'I thought prices had recovered.'

'The best offer they've had is seven thousand less than they want. The agents told 'em that one of the troubles is the rail fares have gone up so much that commuters are hesitating to come this far from London, which means less demand.'

'If their place is worth less than they thought, a bigger house will cost less to buy.'

'Like everyone else, I suppose they were hoping to sell dearly and buy cheaply.'

'This place isn't worth what we've been thinking, then.'

'Since we're not selling, it doesn't matter.'

He stretched out in the chair. 'Tell you one thing, buying this house is the best decision I ever made.'

She would have liked to have reminded him of the days and weeks during which she had done everything in her power to persuade him to buy a home on a mortgage. But being a loving wife, she remained silent.

21

Carr went downstairs, switched on the radio for the news, boiled an egg, made toast and coffee, and noted on the shopping list that he needed marmalade. He'd just put the egg in the egg cup when the phone rang.

'I want some more information.'

The sound of the voice shocked him, but this time did not evoke an immediate sense of self-loathing. He had betrayed himself and the force, but his betrayal had perhaps saved the unborn child and Gloria's reason. It was not an exchange he would have wished to be forced to make, but having made it, he could live with the fact. He pressed the alert button. 'What information?'

'Find out if the police have a lead on Morrell.'

'They've found his body.' He was glad the victim had not been an honest citizen; he was able to avoid making another decision he could not make.

'How d'you know that already – it's not your territory?'

'When I asked about MacClearey, I said a snout had heard the name mentioned and I'd wondered if there were anything to it. After finding Morrell, the Shropshire police have been back on to me to see if my snout has picked up anything more.'

'And?'

'I said he'd heard nothing more than the name at the time and hasn't seen sight or sound of the two men since.'

'Have the coppers up north any leads?'

'I don't know.'

'You'd better hope not.' He cut the connection.

A couple of minutes later, Malicious Calls reported that the call had been made from Euston Station.

He returned to the kitchen, put the egg on the table, ate. He was, he thought bleakly, beginning to learn how a man could admit to a horror and yet not react to it because he isolated the knowledge in his mind. Presumably, that was how the guards in the concentration camps had been able to remain good family men.

George Lumley believed in conspicuous consumption and because he was a jovial John Bull, generous with his time and money, critical of all foreigners and especially of the Frogs, the great British public loved him. When he'd married Lady Sarah, elder daughter of an earl and a not too distant cousin of the Queen, hundreds had gathered outside the church to watch, wave, and wish the couple joy.

He'd made umpteen millions, or a billion, depending on what paper one read, when he'd successfully forecast a coming bear market and sold sackloads of shares he didn't possess; then as much again when he'd successfully forecast a coming bull market and bought sackloads of shares he didn't want. Awash with money, he'd purchased Ullington Castle and turned it from a romantic ruin into a fairy tale, set within a moat and complete with working drawbridge and portcullis.

The party he gave for his daughter on her eighteenth birthday, graced by younger Royals, was so extravagantly magnificent that even the *Guardian* forbore to estimate its cost and equate that with the feeding of starving hundreds in the Third World. The castle and grounds were open to the public on forty days of the year, all admission fees going to charity, and such had been the publicity surrounding the birthday party that on the cold Thursday at the end of January, when normally only relatively few visitors would have been expected, there were almost as many as in June, when the gardens were at their most beautiful.

Trent, dressed casually but expensively, wandered through the public rooms, apparently studying the magnificent furniture, furnishings, and paintings; in fact, noting the security arrangements. He completed his visit by a stroll round the grass border between the castle walls and the moat. He returned to his car, started the engine and drove out of the car park. Difficult, he thought, as he turned on to an A road; bloody difficult. But that, ironically, could be an advantage because the guards – and there could be no doubt that there would be guards on duty throughout the night – would tend to assume that security was too good for anyone to attempt to break in and would, therefore, have become slack.

A hot hatchback raced up to nuzzle the Porsche's exhaust pipe, then nipped past; it was easy to visualize the sneering smile of the young driver. A fool, he thought, was someone who didn't bother to read the odds. He dropped a gear, accelerated, and was doing just short of the ton when he cut across the bows of the hatchback, forcing the other driver to brake fiercely. The manoeuvre put him in a contented mood. So contented that he decided to raise the jackpot to fifteen million. After all, there'd been at least that much hanging on the walls of the castle.

It was impossible to ascertain without making pointed inquiries or risking a visit whether the drawbridge was raised at night. Since to do so would not only have been a good security move, but also the kind of gesture to be expected from a man as flamboyant in nature as Lumley, Trent decided that all planning would be based on the assumption that it would be up. The moat had to be crossed? A small inflatable could be used. Infrared and heat sensors? Heat could be concealed, movement could be slowed until the sensor failed to record it . . . Once inside the castle, they had little to fear because they would use as much force as was necessary. And even if they failed to stifle all alarms, by then it would not matter. The county police force had been so deprived of funds that on a normal night there were only a few cars on the roads and the odds were that they'd arrive far too late; even if, by some chance, the nearest patrol car had been in the vicinity and it reached the scene within minutes, it had to approach along the only road and a short burst from an Uzi would take care of it and its occupants.

Fifteen million pounds. Like winning the lottery. Ten for him, five for the rest of them. Ten million introduced one to the in-places of the world and the in-parties; ten million meant constantly renewing oneself in the fountain of feminine youth.

He began to sing *Celeste Aida*. Though no Domingo, he had a warm, pleasing voice. When still in shorts, a friend of his parents had tried to persuade him to join the church choir, which showed how bloody silly people could be.

Carr parked in front of the nursing home, walked up the slight slope and round to the main entrance. As he went in, a nurse, in conventional uniform, looked over the bannisters, halfway up the curving staircase. 'Evening, Mr Carr.'

Something about her tone alerted him. 'Has it happened?'

'You're the father of a seven pound ten ounces boy. Congratulations!'

He raced up the stairs, shouting his thanks as he passed her, along the corridor, and into the room. Gloria, propped up by pillows, looked tired, but as if she had been touched by grace. He kissed her and as she held him, they said things which if written down would have been nonsense, but which for them had complete meaning.

Eventually, he drew up a chair and sat. 'Where is he?'

'In the nursery.'

'Was it bad?'

'I think I shouted a bit, but I can't really remember.'

'Has he all the right bits and pieces?'

'All present and correct.'

'And you?'

'I don't feel like walking a marathon, but otherwise I'm fine . . . Oh, Mike, it's like a miracle. It makes everything that's happened worthwhile.'

They stole two four-wheel-drive vehicles from different parts of London and drove south at speeds which brought them together a quarter of a mile short of the private road to Ullington Castle.

They parked and two of them left to take care of the couple who lived in the gatehouse. That done – with casual brutality – they turned into the private road and carried on down until they turned off, crossed a field, and parked in the cover of trees and rhododendron bushes. They checked their weapons and equipment, pulled ski masks over their faces, adjusted their tight-knit gloves, left one man to guard their flank with an Uzi, cocked and ready, and carried on down to the moat.

Seen from the ground, the sensors on the outside of the castle walls had looked like standard units, which meant a limited range, but Trent never left anything to chance. When two hundred yards short of the water, he gave the order to drop to the ground and crawl. Each man suffered a familiar urge – to hurry things up so that the job was the sooner completed; each knew that to do so could spell disaster – and forced himself to move slowly. When they reached the water's edge, they used a small bottle of compressed air to inflate their craft.

The wind was light, but even so they dared paddle only so slowly that twice it drove them back before they finally made the far bank. It took them a full twenty minutes to reach the castle wall, hampered by the warmth-retaining capes with which they'd covered themselves.

In the pursuit of visual authenticity, the restoration of the walls had been carried out so that their surface was rough and this gave Nick an easy climb up to the small window, that like all the others nearby was in darkness, but the climb had to be made so slowly that by the time he reached the window, it seemed that every muscle in his body was jumping. He secured himself with a suction safety belt, waited for some of the physical strain to ease, peeled off masking paper from an adhesive pad and pressed the pad against the glass; he used a glass cutter of his own design to draw a rough shape around the pad, then used the padded butt of the cutter to tap the glass until the rectangle broke free. He withdrew the pad, with glass attached, and dropped it into the pouch at his waist.

He took off the right-hand glove, oiled his finger tips so that any print would be hopelessly smeared, reached inside and felt the interior frame of the window. The surface of the wood was smooth and free of any external device; then the alarm trigger was sunk into the plasterwork. Triggers had to be connected to an electrical supply. He checked the surrounding plasterwork and felt a slight irregularity of surface that had length and constant direction. He used a small stone chisel to work unseeing, with the restrained skill of a diamond cutter, to expose the wires. When done, he eased them away from the wall and used a sound-emitting compass – since he could still not see what he was doing – to determine that two of the wires were alive. With the help of cutters, he cross-contacted the live two, cut the remaining two. Both open-circuit and closed-contact alarm systems were now neutralized.

He switched on a torch whose bowl had been masked with tape until it gave little more than a pinprick of light and shone it into the room. Trent had been right. Behind the small window lay the smallest room. He ran the light along the tops of the walls and across the ceiling and saw no alarm point. That made sense – one wouldn't want the

129

alarm's sounding every time someone needed to relieve himself during the night. He opened the window, which swung inwards, and slithered through the small opening into the lavatory. He unwound from about his waist the coil of thin rope, with figure-of-eight knots at regular intervals, secured one end about the base of the lavatory pan, dropped the other through the window, signalled with the torch. That done, he sat on the lavatory and waited, cockily certain that even with the aid of the rope it would take the other two some time to join him; few possessed his monkey-like climbing skills.

They went out of the lavatory into the corridor, knowing that there must be parts of the interior of the castle where the alarms would be active at night, but not bothering to try to identify which ones because it wasn't necessary. If an interior alarm went off when no exterior one had, it was human nature to believe that there could not be an intruder and the system must be at fault, so any response would be delayed and half-hearted. A sleepy, bored, unarmed guard could pose no real threat.

They checked two bedrooms, containing beautiful furniture but no occupant, and were back in the corridor when there were sounds from below. They ranged themselves along the wall, Trent nearest to the huge landing, on which two suits of full armour stood guard. A Dobermann turned into the corridor, head held high as it scented. It opened its mouth to bark. Trent used an aerosol to spray its face. It collapsed to the ground, whimpering, scrabbling desperately at its eyes with its front paws. The guard hurried forward, too concerned for his dog to pause to work out what had happened. A lead-filled cosh on the back of his head knocked him unconscious and fractured his skull.

They resumed their search for occupied bedrooms. All in that corridor proved to be empty, so they retraced their steps and crossed the landing to a second one.

Lumley and Lady Sarah slept in a four poster that was

large enough to leave them looking rather lost. Being the kind of man he was, Lumley tried to scramble out of bed to defend his wife; a blow to the face broke his nose, a knee to his crutch doubled him up, and a kick that was aimed at his jaw but landed on the side of his neck left him helpless. Lady Sarah had time to utter one scream before she was gagged and bound. Turner had a quick fondle of her generous breasts before he followed the others out.

Angelique's room, though considerably smaller than her parents', was huge by any normal standards. Unlike the other bedrooms, it was not filled with beautiful antiques, but with fun pieces and posters, many of which were in doubtful taste; possessions littered the floor. She lay curled up under a single duvet, all that was necessary because of the central heating, and the head of a dachshund was on the pillow next to hers. The dachshund, dim even by the standards of the breed, took time to become alarmed. Before it could bark, it was slammed against the wall so hard that it died instantly. Angelique was a sound sleeper and only woke up completely when the duvet and sheet were ripped back. She was a modern girl and liked short nightdresses, less matching pants; hers had ridden up during sleep, leaving her without any modesty. Instinctively, instead of trying to run, she went to pull down the nightdress.

They taped her mouth and tied her hands and feet and then Turner was left to carry her over his shoulders while the others went on ahead, took out any other guards, and lowered the drawbridge. It was a job Turner greatly enjoyed.

22

As was usual, the police had wanted to contain the news of the kidnapping to enable them to set up aggressive defences, but that proved to be a hopeless ambition; even before they had spoken to Lumley in hospital, one of the Filipino servants, who'd lived long enough in England to sense the degree of loyalty held to be due to an employer, had contacted a national newspaper and been promised a four-figure sum if the truth of what he claimed was verified.

The detective chief superintendent gave his first press conference at three in the afternoon. He was never at ease with the media and he pointed out in aggressive terms that there was as yet no evidence to link this kidnapping with that of Victoria Arkwright and therefore the media must, for the sake of the victim, not try to draw any such conclusion. Moreover, the story must be treated with the greatest possible restraint.

As one of the television reporters said: 'The daughter of one of the richest men in the country and a relation of the Queen is kidnapped by the same mob who raped that other girl silly and he tells us to play it with violets – stupid bastard!'

'I don't understand,' Gloria said. 'How can people be so foul?'

'God knows,' Carr muttered.

'But you must have some idea. You deal with them all the time.'

'The villains we handle are angels compared to this mob.'

'The police will find her in time, won't they?'

'They didn't find Victoria Arkwright.'

'But Angelique's almost a royal.'

He was about to say that in this context social position offered no advantage, but cut the words. Gloria would be far from alone in believing that because of her royal connections, Angelique Lumley must escape the appalling brutality to which Victoria Arkwright had been subjected. But both royal and commoner bled if pricked.

They had rigged a mobile warning system between downstairs and the nursery upstairs and the speaker began to broadcast sounds that were not immediately identifiable. 'He sounds as if he's choking,' she said, as she stood. She hurried out of the room.

He stared into space. He had not given the blackmailer any information that could in any way have assisted this second kidnapping, he could not have provided his superiors with information that would have enabled them to prevent it, yet from the moment the news had broken, he had experienced a self-hatred even more bitter than any felt before . . .

She returned. 'Just gurgling in his sleep.' As she sat, she smiled self-consciously. 'I suppose it'll take time not to panic fifty times a day. It's just that after we've been through so much . . .' She was silent for a moment, then said: 'When I was upstairs and looking down at him and realizing how extraordinary it was that he was there, I began to think of the poor girl. It's agony for her, but it can't be any easier mentally for her parents – perhaps it's even worse in one terrible way because she knows what's happening, they don't and must imagine the very worst. How do people begin to cope with that sort of ghastly situation?'

'If one has to do something, one just does it.'

She looked at him in some surprise. 'But surely circumstances can be so terrible that it all becomes too much?'

'No one's ever found the limits of suffering.'

'That's an odd thing to say. You sound as if . . . Was it that awful for you all the time I was in hospital?'

'Let's drop the subject.'

'I'm sorry.' She was not quite certain for what she was apologizing.

'They should be hanged,' Freda said.

'It's like tiger soup,' Wyatt replied. 'First you've got to catch 'em.'

'And when they're caught, what'll happen? They'll be given a few years in jail and that'll be all and they'll be let out to do it all again. You tell me where's the justice in that? What's the use of the likes of them to the world?'

He said nothing.

'Speak to anyone and they say that sort of people should be hung. So why aren't they?'

'Ask the politicians, not me.'

'They're supposed to do what we want.'

'You've got to be joking. With them, it's kiss the babies before the election, up yours after it.'

'I was talking about it to Hetty in the supermarket. She says, give her the chance and she'll pull up the rope herself.'

'They didn't pull a rope, they opened up a trapdoor.'

'What's it matter? If there were more like her and me, there wouldn't be these awful crimes.'

'But there'd be a lot more hen-pecked husbands.'

'You hen-pecked? You're more like a fattened capon.'

'Steady on.'

She giggled. 'I forgot that they don't have their necessaries.'

They were silent for a while, then she said: 'Hetty was telling me that she saw an advert in the local paper for exactly the house they want. She went back to the estate agent and asked if their place had increased in value by

134

much. He told her that if anything, it had gone down. And when she said what I'd told her, that the manager of Mike's building society had given him a second mortgage because prices had gone up, the estate agent said that if the manager did all his business like that, the society would very soon be bust.' She yawned. 'I'm tired. I'm going to bed.'

'There's that programme on the telly at ten-thirty.'

'That's all right. You stay down and watch it.'

She left the room. He checked the time. Twenty past ten. He stared across the room. Only the Lumley family knew how savagely they were suffering, but he could appreciate a little of their pain because he had talked to women who had been raped and to parents whose children were missing and he had seen the agony in their eyes. He hated the men of violence every bit as keenly as did Freda, but he was too much of a realist to believe that capital punishment would return. Those in power had for too long been beguiled by the siren songs of the liberals who could command public attention and who did not have to live near the real world where crime caused untold suffering. A kidnapping always faced the police with the need to make an impossible choice. The family wanted the victim back at the first possible moment, the police wanted time to plan, to follow up every clue however insignificant, to stretch the kidnappers' nerves to the point where they might make a mistake. Yet time had not saved Victoria. How could the parents of Angelique meet the advice of the police not to pay the ransom immediately it was demanded when they must realize that not to do so must place her at risk of suffering similar appalling degradations to those that Victoria had? Could any parent hesitate and agree to follow the police's advice? . . . Grant had said that his DCS was projecting the possibility that a policeman was working with the blackmailing mob. Some senior officers were ignorant bastards, incapable of realizing that no policeman could ever begin to consider working with such scum, whatever his reason for doing so . . . Mike's contact had overheard two loudmouths mention MacClearey, presumably because of a proposed kidnapping that for whatever reason had not taken place, which meant that if only contact could have been made with them, vital information regarding the identities of the kidnappers might have been eased out of them – one way or another. Odd they should have been so voluble when the kidnapping of Victoria had shown the mob to be really tightly run, so that one would have expected them to keep their mouths shut in public places . . . His mind began to drift as he closed his eyes. Another odd thing was the way in which Mike's house had increased in value when it seemed every other one in Everden hadn't . . . He opened his eyes, sat upright, and silently cursed himself because into his mind had swept a shocking possibility. And it was no good his trying to excuse himself on the grounds that it was his job to be suspicious, since only a moment before he'd been criticizing Grant's D C S for disloyal suspicions. The next thing would be, he'd start wondering who Freda entertained when he was at the station . . .

He stood, turned off the television at the plug, left the room. He checked that the front door was locked, the windows were secured, the back door was locked. He went upstairs. The bedroom was in darkness, so he began to edge his way round the end of the bed, able to judge the route exactly because of the many times he'd returned in the middle of the night.

'It's all right,' she said. 'I only turned the light off a moment ago.' She switched on the wall light above her side of the double bed. 'Was it a good programme?'

'How's that?'

'Was the programme worth staying up for?'

'I didn't watch it.' He reached under the pillows for his pyjamas.

'Fell asleep, I suppose.'

'I was thinking and kind of forgot.' He began to undress. 'Remember you were going to see Gloria one day, but couldn't because something turned up and so you nipped round to their place later on and asked Mike to take the fruit and he said to phone Gloria and have a word with her – when you told me, you mentioned he'd had a Caller Display unit installed, didn't you?'

'It was the first I'd seen.'

'And you mentioned another bit of equipment which you wondered what it was for?'

'Did I?'

'You can't remember?'

She shook her head.

He climbed into bed. She usually read before sleeping, he never did. 'You can switch the light off.'

'Aren't you going to kiss me goodnight?'

He kissed her, with deep affection and complete lack of passion.

She switched off the light. He thought about his retirement. A cruise to celebrate it? He knew what her reaction would be to any such suggestion. Spend that much money on themselves for just a few days? . . . Images of ships, sea, and conch shells began to drift through his mind.

'I've just remembered,' she said.

'I was just falling asleep.'

'Sorry, but you did ask and I've been trying hard to think back. There was another little black box by the side of the telephone and it had just a yellow button on it.'

The description was too vague for him to be certain, yet he'd little doubt that what she'd seen had been an alert unit, supplied by the bureau. Carr had not requested the bureau's help through official channels as he would have done had he been receiving anonymous calls that were connected with some case he was handling and which needed to be traced, so why had the two units been installed? Those ugly, disloyal suspicions returned to make certain sleep did not come quickly.

23

Wyatt despised himself for his suspicions, but they would not disappear. He reached across the desk for the phone, withdrew his hand. He stood, walked over to the window and stared across the street at the leafless sweet chestnut trees that ringed the vicarage garden on the opposite side. Mike might have had cause to ask for an alert unit and forgotten to log his request. There might well be something special about his house or the area that was responsible for an increase in value that was not universal. And, above all, what conceivable motive could there be to cause him to act so completely out of character? Honesty compelled Wyatt to admit the answer to that last question. In hospital, Gloria had become so depressed that there had been fears for the safety of her unborn child and of herself. Carr had been convinced – rightly as it turned out – that if only she could be moved to a nursing home, she would recover from the depression. He had been desperate to find the money to move her.

Wyatt returned to the desk, sat, lifted the receiver, dialled the Malicious Calls bureau and when the connection was made, gave the reason for his call.

'That's right. We installed the two units last month.'

'For what reason?'

'Why d'you think? Because they were requested.'

'Sure. But what reason for the request was given?'

'Hang on.'

Wyatt drummed on the desk with his fingers. This call

had to be arousing the other's curiosity. Pray God that such curiosity didn't spill out and fuel anyone else's suspicions . . .

'Detective Constable Carr said he'd been receiving certain calls and needed to know who was making them. The installation was OK'd by his superior.'

'Who was that?'

'Detective Inspector Hoskin. What's the problem? The right hand doesn't know where the left hand is, let alone what it's doing?'

'Something like that.'

After replacing the receiver, he continued to drum on the desk. Mike might have had a genuine reason for the request, Hoskin might have OK'd it, no one remembered to log the facts. Whether that were so was very easily determined – ask the DI. But to do that would be to expose Mike to an open suspicion of guilt . . . Wyatt realized he was allowing friendship to blind him to the fact that if Mike had sold himself, he might well have information that would identify the kidnappers and therefore the possibility that he would suffer the trauma of being unjustly suspected could be of no consequence whatsoever.

He left the station and drove up to the High Street and then halfway down Gower Street to the new Sainsbury's, on top of which was an open car park. From there, he walked back to the High Street and into an estate agent whose trade was mainly in the low to middle price bracket.

The receptionist showed him into an office in which worked a woman, younger than he, smartly presented and professionally brisk. She asked him how she could help. He explained.

'I think I need to know the exact area if I'm to be reasonably accurate.'

'Watts Road,' he answered reluctantly, as if even to name the road would identify Carr.

She thought for a moment. 'I seem to remember . . .' She swivelled her chair round and brought out a box file from a cabinet. She opened the file, checked through the papers inside, brought out two pages clipped together. She skimmed through the pages. 'I thought so,' she said, not without a trace of satisfaction. 'Three years ago, we handled a house in Chepstowe Lane, which is immediately behind Watts Road, and sold it for forty-one thousand. It came back on the market in May at sixty thousand, even though we advised the owner that in the current market, that was an unrealistic price. There were a few inquiries, but no offers, and as the owner's job had moved up north and he wanted his family up there, but they couldn't be until he sold, he agreed to bring the price down. The house finally found a buyer at forty-eight thousand.'

'So it's unlikely that someone who has to know about property values would accept that a house in Watts Road had increased its value by more than three thousand pounds in the recent past?'

'Very unlikely.'

He thanked her for her help, left. He had to accept that he was faced by an irony. The negation of his suspicions would clear Mike, yet the proof of them might point the way to evidence that would identify the kidnappers.

The building society's branch office was halfway along the High Street, in one of the oldest buildings which, thanks to an unusually responsible attitude, had had its exterior repaired but left unaltered and its interior modernized in such a way as not to destroy character.

The middle-aged manager had a quick smile, a firm handshake, and a manner that was straightforward, but often strangely formal.

'I understand,' Wyatt said, 'that your predecessor retired at the end of last year.'

'He retired nearly five years ago.' He studied Wyatt. 'My answer seems to disturb you?'

'Only because . . . Frankly, my inquiry is both difficult and confidential.'

'So you said at the beginning. Perhaps if I point out that the ability to respect confidences is an integral part of my job?'

'This is . . . different.'

'If you could be more explicit?'

'Michael Carr has a mortgage with you.'

'Without checking, I cannot comment, but for the moment I'll accept that.'

'I need to know whether at the end of last year he was granted a second mortgage for three thousand pounds.'

The manager began to stroke his square chin with his thumb. 'You have a court order calling on me to divulge the information?'

'No.'

'Then you must know I cannot give it without the client's permission.'

'It takes time to get an order.'

'That has to be a matter for you, not me.'

'The information could save someone from being murdered.'

The manager dropped his hand away from his chin. 'You're not exaggerating?'

'I wish I were.'

'And someone may be put in even greater jeopardy if I insist on a court order?'

'Yes.'

He studied the far wall. He fidgeted with the corner of a sheet of paper on the desk. 'Very well,' he finally said. 'If I have your word that what you've told me is fact?'

'You have it.'

Less than five minutes later, Wyatt learned that Carr had applied for a second mortgage and this had been refused because his house did not hold sufficient value.

* * *

142

The drive to the Hoskins' house had Wyatt questioning his move time and time again; a less stubborn man might well have turned round.

Miranda opened the front door. 'Hullo, Sergeant Wyatt.'

Virtually every time he met her, he wondered whether Freda was wholly right and Miranda's manner was the result of shyness and not an overwhelming sense of superiority. 'Is the guv'nor in, Mrs Hoskin?'

'I'm afraid he isn't at the moment.'

'When do you expect him back?'

'Very soon.'

'Would you mind if I waited for him?'

She hesitated. 'He is very tired. Couldn't the matter wait until tomorrow?'

'I'm afraid not.'

'Then you'd better come in.' As he entered, she said: 'Don't forget to mind your head.'

'I won't.'

'It's turned quite cold, hasn't it? And the forecast said that snow's possible later in the week.'

He ducked under the lintel and entered the sitting room. The two children were watching the television and when she told them to turn it off and go through to the kitchen and watch the set in there, they looked at Wyatt with undisguised resentment as they left. She offered him a drink, poured it, and talked about the social life of the division, asking him for his opinion on the proposed changes in the annual dinner dance. Since she appeared to believe it was popular, he found great difficulty in giving any sort of an opinion. Conversation had become difficult by the time they heard the sound of the front door's being opened and closed.

'There's Bevis,' she said, not quite concealing her relief.

Hoskin entered. 'I thought it was your old banger parked outside. My God, but the wind's beginning to get knives in it!'

143

'Would you like a drink?' she asked.

'As I'm not doing any more driving, a really stiff whisky, but I'll get it.'

'Better make it a small one, Guv,' Wyatt said.

'Trouble?'

'Could be. In six foot high capitals.'

'Then we'll go through to the other room.'

The study was a small, heavily beamed room with a single window. Comfort was the theme, not smart chic. The easy chair had seen hard wear, the desk was an antique only in age, not value, the carpet had several stains, and the curtains were too short. Hoskin sat on the edge of the desk. 'So what's got you looking like a man who's lost the winning lottery ticket?'

'It's . . . it's difficult to know how to begin.'

'Try at the beginning.'

'It's possible Mike Carr's been grassing to the mob who've snatched the Lumley girl,' Wyatt said in a rush of words.

'Have you gone bloody mad?'

'No.'

'Shit! . . . Let's have it, then.'

Hoskin listened without once interrupting, then said, voice harsh: 'Most of that's supposition or circumstantial.'

'If you'd seen his expression when he learned Shropshire were asking about MacClearey and again when I told him Morrell had been tortured and murdered.'

'It obviously didn't say anything to you at the time and it's only now when you find either occasion significant. Damnit, you know as well as me that expressions can be the biggest liars out.'

'He was desperate to find some way of affording to move Gloria.'

'Who wouldn't have been?'

'Where did the money come from?'

'Have you asked him?'

'I've only now confirmed the fact that he didn't obtain

144

a second mortgage, as he's told everyone, including his wife.'

'Then you're quick to slag the man!'

'The facts . . .'

'You're saying that an officer who's proved himself to be keen, efficient, intelligent, and straight, suddenly decides to turn crook; that knowing what the mob did to Victoria Arkwright, he nevertheless is ready to work with them.'

'I know him well enough to be certain it can't have been voluntarily.'

'Goddamnit, you've been saying just that.'

'What I mean, sir, is that he'd never have intended things. But once he couldn't avoid working for them for whatever reason, he used the money they paid to help Gloria.'

'In other words, the mob had something on him and used this to force him to grass. What's that something?'

'I don't know.'

'There's a sight more you don't know than that you do.'

'Surely there is one certainty? If he's been working with the mob, he should be able to provide a lead?'

'Which you imagine he'll willingly pass on after making a full confession because of delayed conscience?'

'It could happen.'

'Only in once-upon-a-time land . . . Use that phone there to ring him and tell him to get to the station now.'

24

Carr replaced the receiver. Something big might have occurred that had nothing to do with the kidnapping; something big might have occurred that was connected to the kidnapping, but in no way directly involved him; but he sensed with icy fear that he was under suspicion.

'Who was it?' Gloria called from the kitchen.

'I've got to get back to the station.'

'Now?'

''Fraid so.'

She appeared in the doorway. 'But you haven't been back half an hour.'

He shrugged his shoulders.

'Is something wrong?'

'Why d'you ask?'

'You look as if . . . Well, as if something worrying has happened.'

'It has. My supper's going to be delayed.'

'That really is all?'

'May I be turned from a handsome prince into a frog if I'm lying.'

She smiled. 'You're getting ideas above your appearance.' Then, her smile gone, she said: 'You promise me nothing's happened?'

Before he could answer, there was a wail through the loudspeaker in the kitchen that sent her hurrying upstairs. For once he was grateful for a son with powerful lungs.

He drove to the end of the road, turned right, right

again at the T-junction, and drew up by a call box. He'd known too many cases where well-laid plans had gone astray through unforeseen circumstances not to have worked out an emergency plan. He inserted a call card, dialled. His mother answered. He sympathized with her latest aches and pains and the neighbours who would keep shouting, promised the family would be up to see her very soon, said: 'Mum, d'you remember me asking you a little while back to support me if that became neessary?'

'Naturally I do.'

'Also that I told you how you could help?'

'I may never see sixty again, but I'm not quite in my dotage yet.'

'Of course you're not. Then it's to say you lent me the three thousand.'

'Very well, dear. And who'll be asking me?'

'Detective Inspector Hoskin.'

'I met him at one of your parties. Rather a nice man, isn't he?'

'Part of the time.'

A couple of minutes later, he said goodbye and rang off. She had shown no curiosity. A loving mother, she believed in him implicitly, and would never doubt him. Which showed how wrong loving mothers could be.

In the station, he parked alongside the DI's Mondeo. The DI was sharp, but fair and because he offered those under him the same degree of loyalty he expected them to show, he would be very reluctant to believe one of his DCs had turned crook. So play on that reluctance . . .

He took the lift up to the fourth floor, conscious of rising tension and fear. He believed he had covered himself, but didn't every criminal think that before he was arrested.

Hoskin sat behind his desk, Wyatt stood by the window. The desk light had the effect of drawing shadows on the DI's face which highlighted the harshness of some of his features. 'Sit down.'

147

Carr sat on the chair in front of the desk.

'You know why you're here, of course.'

First rule of interrogation. Make the suspect believe you know more than you do; first defence of the suspect, admit nothing. 'On the contrary, sir, I have no idea.'

'Come on, don't waste my time.'

'If it isn't impertinent, I'd like to ask if perhaps you aren't wasting the time of both of us?'

That annoyed Hoskin, but also elicited very brief, professional respect.

'Very well. Did you request British Telecom to instal a Caller Display and an alert unit at your home?'

'To be precise, I asked them to take whatever steps were necessary to trace certain incoming calls and they decided on the equipment.'

'Did you make out the usual requisition note?'

'Of course.'

'In whose name?'

'Yours, sir.'

'In whose name did you sign it?'

'Yours, sir.'

'An act of forgery, since I know nothing about the request.'

'In theory, I suppose it could be called that. But it's not so long ago I told you a similar authorization needed your signature and you said to sign it in your name because you were busy and the form would only be filed along with all the others no one ever read.'

'Why did you want your calls monitored?'

'To find out if their place of origin would help determine who was making them.'

'This is in connection with what?'

'As yet, no definite case. The caller is a man who refuses to identify himself, but is offering to grass heavy.'

'Sergeant Wyatt says you have not logged anything.'

'There seemed no point in doing so until I became

reasonably certain that the caller is genuine and not trying to moonshine me. I'm still undetermined.'

'He also says you failed to log the fact that you had been given a possible lead on the Arkwright kidnapping.'

'Presumably, you're referring to the fact that I was given word two newcomers to the patch had been talking about MacClearey. Initially, that name meant nothing to me. However, after learning the facts from Sergeant Grant, I got back on to my source and told him to find the couple and listen in, but he's not seen them again. There just didn't seem to be anything to log.'

'Sergeant Grant asked you to get back on to him; you didn't.'

'Get back if I learned anything more.'

'Sergeant Wyatt says that when you heard that the MacClearey household might be the target for a second kidnapping, you were horrified.'

'Naturally.'

'I should have thought that the immediate reaction of any officer would be excitement, since this raised the possibility of gaining a lead on the kidnappers.'

'My horror of any repetition of the suffering of Victoria Arkwright momentarily outweighed my excitement at the possibility of fingering the villains.'

'At the end of last year, your wife was in hospital, suffering from a form of eclampsia and an accompanying deep depression.'

'I fail to see that that can have the slightest relevancy.'

'And her depression became so severe that there were fears for the safety not only of the child but of her. Unfortunately, the doctors decided that because of the child, they could not treat her with sufficiently strong anti-depressants. Is that correct?'

'Yes.'

'And you believed that the only feasible solution was to move her to a private nursing home?'

'Yes.'

'Did you ask the building society with whom you had the original mortgage for a second mortgage?'

'Yes.'

'And did they grant it to you?'

'The manager explained that the rules of the building society would not allow him to lend me any more in view of the drop in property values, even though he very much wished that because of the special circumstances, he could.'

'Am I right in understanding that despite this fact, you told your wife the building society had granted you a second mortgage and it was this that would pay for the nursing home?'

'You are.'

'And that is what you also said to Sergeant Wyatt?'

'It is.'

'Why did you lie?'

'Embarrassment.'

'Explain.'

'I became more and more desperate as Gloria's depression deepened. One day, my mother rang and she guessed that something was very wrong and asked what was the trouble. I told her. She immediately said she'd lend me the money. I tried to refuse, but . . .' He became silent.

'The circumstances being as you've described them, why did you think of refusing?'

'After my father died, my mother was left with only a little capital and her pension. If she lent me three thousand, obviously her income would go down. Not by much, but when one's not well off to begin with, a little becomes a lot . . . I decided I couldn't tell Gloria the truth because she knew what my mother's financial position was and the knowledge that because of her my mother would have to make do with even less must inevitably upset her, maybe even to the extent that it would negate any value the move gave. So I told her I'd obtained a second mortgage – there was no way she'd find out that

150

that was a lie while she was in the nursing home. And once I'd told her that, I couldn't give the sarge a different version in case he mentioned it to Freda and Freda spoke about it to Gloria.'

'Do you have any objection to my confirming the loan with your mother?'

'I object like hell.'

'Why?'

'She would hate to think that the news had become public property.'

'Hardly very public. In any case, you know how we work.'

'You feel just about as much loyalty for your DCs as Maxwell did for his pensioners.'

'Cut that out,' Wyatt said sharply.

'I can be accused of tying in with a mob of raping, torturing, murdering bastards, but I'm not allowed even to criticize my accuser?'

'No one's accused you of anything.'

'You've brought me here for the pleasure of my company?'

'Let me put the question slightly differently,' said Hoskin. 'Will you agree to my telephoning your mother and asking her to confirm what you've just told us concerning the loan?'

'Have I an option? If I don't, presumably you'll arrest me.'

'What is the number?'

He gave it.

Hoskin dialled. 'Mrs Carr, this is Inspector Hoskin . . . Indeed, I remember . . . My wife is fine, thanks very much. Would you . . . That's very kind of you. I'm sorry to have to ask you this, but circumstances make it necessary and I can assure you that your answer will be treated as confidentially as possible. Have you in the past two or three months lent your son any money? . . . Exactly how much? . . . I understand the improvement in Mrs Carr was little short of miraculous . . . No, I'm afraid I haven't seen the baby yet . . . Thank you very much for your help . . . And I look forward to meeting you again, Mrs Carr. Goodbye.' He replaced the receiver. 'Your mother confirms that she lent you three thousand pounds.'

'That must disappoint you.'

'When one is in command, one sometimes has to do something that one would very much rather not. It was my duty to question you, whatever my personal feelings, first because certain facts had to be explained, far more importantly to discover if you knew anything that might give a lead to the identity or the whereabouts of the kidnappers.'

'It obviously didn't occur to you that if I had, I'd have rushed to tell you.'

'I can only repeat what I've just said.'

There was silence.

'Is that all?' Carr asked.

'For the moment.'

He left. He found it impossible to judge how far they had believed him.

25

When Carr awoke, the bedroom was in half light, and, convinced he'd slept through the alarm, he jumped out of bed. Only then did he check the time to discover there was a quarter of an hour before he need get up. He crossed to the window and pulled the curtain; during the night, there had been a fall of snow.

He went through to the nursery where Gloria was sleeping so that she could soothe and feed Timothy without his being woken, kissed her good morning, looked into the cot at the sleeping baby, said: 'It's snowed during the night.'

'The forecast last night mentioned snow showers.'

'From up here it looks much heavier than that. You can't tell where the flower beds end and the lawn begins.'

'So what's different?'

'I'll treat that with the contempt it deserves.'

'Never mind, my love, even if you aren't an enthusiastic gardener, you're a perfect husband.'

'For that, I'm your slave. So can I cook you eggs and bacon?'

'Perhaps just one egg and one rasher of bacon as long as it's not fatty.'

Downstairs, he prepared breakfast, gaining satisfaction from the fact that for once the toast was made as the eggs and bacon were cooked and as the coffee machine hissed.

He stepped into the hall. 'Grub's up!'

She came down, Timothy in her arms and mewling

half-heartedly. She put him down in the carrycot and gave him the strip of red velvet that had become a comforter. Almost immediately, he became silent as he slept. She sat at the small kitchen table. 'Who'd have thought?'

'Thought what?' he asked, as he put a plate in front of her.

'That life could be this perfect.'

He had finished his two eggs and three rashers of bacon and was eating a second piece of toast and marmalade when the phone rang.

'It has to be the station this early,' she said angrily. 'Can't they even let you have breakfast in peace?'

'Right now, it's all panic stops out.'

'Because of the kidnapping?'

He nodded.

'What can any of you do when it happened in another county?'

'Sweep up every snout and promise him a fortune if he comes up good, and broken bones if he doesn't.' He hurried through to the hall, lifted the receiver.

'What's the news?'

It was not a voice he recognized. 'What about?'

'You're dumb, even for a split!'

He realized he was being dumb. So dumb that he'd fooled himself into thinking that they would leave him alone because they had milked him of all they wanted. The Caller Display unit was blank; he pressed the yellow button on the alert unit.

'Is anyone in the frame, stupid?'

This voice could hardly have been more dissimilar to the voice of the man who had always previously phoned. Instead of mockery and a sense of perverted pleasure, it projected aggression and hatred. 'I don't know. It's another force carrying out the investigation.'

'You must have heard something.'

'We've heard nothing. Which must mean, there's nothing to hear.'

154

'You'd better hope it stays that way, cholentz.' The line went dead.

'Was it the station?' Gloria called out.

'A snout. Trying to sell news that's useless.'

'Then come on through and finish your breakfast.'

Before he could move, Malicious Calls told him that the call had come from a public box in Gorton Street, Manchester. After replacing the receiver, he walked across to the doorway of the kitchen. 'I'm on my way.'

'You're not going anywhere until you've finished eating,' she said.

'There's not the time.'

'On a day like this, Mike Carr, you're not leaving until you've had a really good meal. And if Mr Hoskin complains because you're twenty seconds late, refer him to me.'

He entered, sat, put more marmalade on the toast. She'd switched on the radio and the news was on. There had been moderate to heavy falls of snow, very localized, and due to strong winds there was drifting in places. Some commuter trains had been badly delayed and it was not expected that regular services could be resumed until the afternoon. Although most main roads were open, many country lanes were blocked and drivers were warned to take very great care. A woman in labour had been airlifted to hospital just in time for her baby to be born there . . .

'It's the same every year,' Gloria said, 'but it always comes as a complete surprise. If this were Canada, we'd all go into hibernation for the winter . . . If you have to go anywhere by car, you will take care, won't you?'

It seemed a bit late to be careful.

Carr entered the CID general room to find Atkin and Buckley present. He muttered a good morning, crossed to his desk, sat.

Atkin was his usual ebullient self. 'I had half a mind to phone in sick and go skiing.'

155

'You never have more than half a mind to do anything with,' Buckley said. 'And where are you going to go skiing round here – the council park?'

'Lamont Hill. It may not be the Cresta Run, but it's good for a bit of a ski.'

'The Cresta Run is for tobogganing.'

'Trivial Pursuits must be hiring you as a consultant . . . Make yourself useful for a change and tell me, if you had a real prospect lined up, where would you take her for an intimate meal?'

'Home.'

'I suggested that. She turned the idea down flat.'

'Shows she's some common sense even if she is friendly with you.'

'I promised to behave myself.'

'She obviously knows you're a liar.'

'I never lie to a lady unless she wants me to in order to surrender with a clear conscience. Come on, you must know somewhere good and cheap.'

'They're either good *or* cheap, never both.'

'What a miserable bastard you can be.'

'It's that what keeps me happy.'

Atkin turned. 'Hey, Mike, where can I take her?'

Carr jerked his mind away from black thoughts. 'What's the matter?'

'I want to know somewhere that doesn't cost an arm and a leg that I can take my latest to and have a good meal in a warming ambience.'

'I wouldn't know.'

'You're an even more miserable bastard. The trouble with you married blokes is that you can get it without having to spend a fortune each time. Come on, pull the mufflers out of your brains and tell me somewhere.'

'Try the Bricklayers Arms. The fixed meal is twelve quid.'

'Including wine?'

'You believe in miracles? But a pretty good Spanish red will only set you back another six quid.'

156

'And it's the kind of place that makes a lady feel good?'

'Candles on the table and an open wood fire.'

'Just what the doctor ordered. Candles get women romantic and ready to believe whatever you tell 'em. Where is this pub?'

'Bedlington.'

'Bedlington? You dozy sod! I thought you were talking about the town. Bedlington's six miles out.'

'It's better when you have to work for it.'

'You think I'm pulling a sledge for six miles? Hasn't anyone told you? The country roads round here are in a hell of a state and more snow's forecast. Only a bloody fool's going to go anywhere outside the town.'

'So when are you off?' asked Buckley.

Atkin stood, picked up a file, left.

The words repeated themselves in Carr's mind as they gathered a significance that would have astonished Atkin. 'Only a bloody fool's going to go anywhere outside the town.'

'Meet him,' said Buckley, jerking his thumb in the direction of the door, 'and you meet a one-track ambition.'

Carr ignored the comment. Because man welcomed an ordered world, he preferred routine to randomness; criminals were no exception and frequently became slaves to a successful routine, superstitiously fearing that the slightest deviation from it would promote disaster. Hence the close attention by the police to the modus operandi of any crime. The first blackmailer, obviously enjoying the opportunity to debase a policeman, had made all previous calls from London termini. Yet this second man had projected hatred rather than enjoyment and had used a Manchester call box. Why the change in routine; why had the original man forgone a further chance to humiliate?

Carr looked through the nearer window. On the road and pavements, the snow had either melted or had been turned into dirty mush, but on the roof, window ledges, trees and bushes of the vicarage and its gardens, it remained. The country lanes would be difficult to traverse even where they were not blocked by drifts; ploughs had a habit of heaping snow across a drive and completely sealing it . . .

'Just tell me something, have you joined the Trappists?'

Early in his career, a grizzled sergeant had said that with his imagination, he should be in politics, not the police. But sometimes it was difficult to draw a line between imagination and an intelligent projection from known facts . . . However experienced a criminal might be, invariably he suffered tension not only throughout the execution of a crime, but also afterwards when he was waiting to discover whether the police were on his trail. The blackmailer would have suffered the urge to discover whether there was any danger to him, an urge ironically becoming ever stronger because he enjoyed a way of finding out the answer. Normally he would have followed the routine that ensured him complete safety and have phoned from a London terminus. But something had prevented his doing that. Had that something been an unexpected snowfall that had closed country lanes? Criminals were subject to many superstitions and one of those most generally held was that even a slight glitch could be the harbinger of disaster. When he had realized that if he wanted to phone from London he would have to wait, perhaps for days, he had suffered a premonition of disaster on top of the already acute tension. So, by now desperate to know, he had phoned a contact in Manchester and told him to get on to D C Carr . . .

Buckley, causing as much noise as possible, left the room, resentfully slamming the door behind himself.

The snow had been very localized. For a house to be snowbound, it must be in the countryside. That still left God knows how many houses in which the kidnapper might be, and his captive, letting time put ever more pressure on the distraught parents; far too many houses for any thorough search to be a feasible possibility . . .

There had to be something more; some further fact that would identify the individual house. He would not believe that he had learned this much, but could learn nothing more; he took aboard a superstition of his own – because he had betrayed unwillingly, he was being offered through his betrayal the chance to save Angelique Lumley.

Mrs Gladwin, who lived in flat 2, 36 Egremont Road, had seen two men going up the stairs on that Monday. She'd been unable to describe them beyond the fact that the elder man had been well built, dressed in an expensive-looking fawn camel's-hair overcoat, and had had black, curly hair. At the time, her description had reminded him of the man whom he had seen leaving the house on a previous occasion. Neither then nor now, though, could there be the certainty that they were the same man. But accept that they were – and the blackmailer must have been one of Genevieve's frequent customers – and one could postulate that he lived in the snow-filled areas of the countryside and ran a silver Porsche. To trace the owner of such a car was not an impossible task . . .

He cursed. In his growing excitement, he had over-looked one fact. There could be no search unless he admitted all the facts.

26

No matter how his mind twisted and turned, the equation did not alter. Confession must result in conviction and imprisonment. If it turned out that all his deductions were fiction, he would have sacrificed everything for nothing. Yet silence meant that Angelique's imprisonment would not only continue, but might end in the appalling nightmare Victoria Arkwright had suffered . . .

It was no contest. Not now Gloria and Timothy were no longer at risk. As he left the CID general room, he grimly compared himself to a man on the way to the scaffold – calling on someone, something to postpone the hanging, yet knowing that nothing would and so wishing it were over.

He was halfway to the DI's room when he came to an abrupt halt. He had been betrayed by his own weakness. Wasn't it just possible that another man could be betrayed by his? Possibilities raced through his mind; hope began to grow . . .

He continued along the corridor, knocked, entered. Hoskin, reading some papers, looked up. 'Well?'

'I'd like a word, sir.' He shut the door with his foot, advanced to the desk. 'I may know enough to provide a lead on the kidnappers.'

'Christ!' Initial excitement gave way to doubt and suspicion.

'The only thing is, I'm wondering whether to make my report to you or to the detective chief superintendent.'

'Have you gone bloody mad?'

'It's just that you might be more ready to come to an agreement.'

'Over what?'

'Over arranging things to everyone's satisfaction.'

'Sergeant Wyatt was right.' Hoskin slammed his fist down on the desk. 'He was bloody right! You, a copper, have been working with those bastards.'

'Sometimes a man has to choose between two courses of action, whatever the consequences.'

'Not in my bloody book.'

'That's a pity. Because if you did decide that that was possible, you would go on to accept that just occasionally the end does justify the means.'

'Talk straight.'

'I can give my information to Mr Jameson or I can give it to you. If I give it to him, he'll have me arrested on the spot and then check out my information; if that proves to be good and he finds Angelique Lumley, he'll make the headlines while you'll be the D C who loses all chance of promotion because you've had a bent D C in your command and not realized the fact. Tough, but that's the way things work. Or I can give the information to you now on the condition that if it turns out to be good and you become the headline news and have promotion chasing you, instead of the other way around, you support me while if it turns out to be bad, you dump me and for my part, I keep my mouth shut. You stand to gain; you can't lose.'

'Agree to that and I climb down to your level.'

'The choice never comes easily. Perhaps, though, you don't see that there can be a choice because you're a man of honour. For you, there can be no contract with the dishonourable, no matter what the cost to yourself. For you, the loss of all chance of promotion cannot be set in the scales against the satisfaction to be gained from knowing that your honour remains unsullied . . . I admire the strength of such principles, even while failing to understand them.'

Hoskin, his face expressing contradictory emotions, stood, crossed to the window, looked out. 'If I made such an agreement, I'd not only be betraying my duty, I'd be placing myself at risk.'

'I've said, if my information proves to be dud, I'll forget there's ever been an agreement between us.'

'You expect me to accept the word of a traitor?'

'What would I gain by breaking it? And if there's no written proof, all you would need to do is claim I was lying, trying to get my own back because you'd exposed me. In the circumstances, how much weight do you think my word would carry against yours?'

Hoskin returned to his seat. He fiddled with the end of his nose. 'Get out.' His tone was bitter, not angry.

The internal phone on Lock's desk rang. Pettit, one desk away, answered it. He called out: 'Mike, the guv'nor wants you.'

Carr left and went down the corridor to the DI's office. Hoskin, sitting at his desk, said, his voice harsh: 'Shut the door.' There was a long pause. 'Facts are facts. There's nothing I can do to alter them.'

'But you can twist them.'

'How?'

'By testifying that the moment the mob contacted me, I informed you of the fact; that you then instructed me to appear to give in to their blackmailing while in fact passing on no useful information, in the hopes of learning something that would give us a lead on them.'

'What put you in a position to be blackmailed?'

'They photographed me in compromising circumstances and threatened to send photos to Gloria. They knew as well as I what effect that would have had on her.'

'You're saying you were screwing around when she was in hospital?'

162

'I'm not proud of the fact.'

'I'm surprised,' said Hoskin, with fresh contempt.

'It's easy to be high-minded when you're on the outside looking in. I was on the inside. And Genevieve made all the running.'

'But you were careful not to run quite as fast as her.'

There was a silence, which Carr broke. 'Do you agree?'

'What's the evidence?'

He took that to be acceptance of the deal. He briefly gave the facts.

'That's all?' said Hoskin.

'I've known cases cracked on far less.'

'And I've known cases where there's been far more end up in the dead file.'

'But if there's one chance in a hundred that we can trace them . . .'

Hoskin interrupted angrily. 'I don't bloody need you to show the way. You didn't notice anything more about the Porsche other than that it was a silver nine-eleven coupé; no special feature to help identify it more exactly?'

'I only gave it a cursory glance.'

'New?'

'Probably new or newish, but some owners cosset their cars so much that you can't really judge age when the model hardly changes.'

'Delineate the area that's been snowbound, then get on to Swansea and tell 'em we want a list of owners who live in it. They'll have a moan because they're geared to give information from names or registration numbers, but tell 'em lives depend on our knowing, fast.'

Carr left. Hoskin's expression was more bitter than ever.

Miranda watched her husband refill his glass — his fourth drink of the evening when normally he had only one. Her sense of worry, which had arisen as soon as he'd arrived home and she'd sensed his inner turmoil, grew. She stood, crossed to his chair, sat on the arm of that, and snuggled against him. 'Has it been a bad day?'

'Bloody awful.'

'I wish you'd learn to take things more easily.'

He said nothing.

'Are you going to tell me why it's been so grim?'

He emptied the glass with three quick swallows. 'If you really must know, I stared into a looking glass and hated what I saw.'

She stroked the side of his neck. 'If you'd looked properly, you'd have seen someone to be proud of because he cares a damn sight more about the world than most. You can't do everything. You can't take on board every other person's pain.'

'This time, it's all mine.'

'Why?'

He went to drink, found the glass empty. He started to rise, but she put her hand on his shoulder and pressed him down. 'Please tell me.'

'Forget it.'

'No, I won't.'

'I'm not Cromwell.'

'I don't understand.'

'I'd rather the warts were left off my portrait.'

'Remember when we were first married, we promised we'd tell each other everything however much we wanted to hide it because that was the only way it could be an honest marriage?'

'Newlyweds are notoriously naive.'

'Are you . . . ?' Without realizing the fact, she gripped his shoulder. 'Are you trying to tell me you're having an affair?'

'For God's sake! How the hell can you think that?'

'Only with terrible pain. But if it's not that, why can't you tell me what the trouble is?'

He spoke slowly and reluctantly. 'I've always played

things dead straight, because that's the only way if there's to be true law and justice. Take a short cut and there's no knowing where one will end up. I've kicked out good men who took short cuts because they thought the ends were more important than the means.'

'You've taken a short cut?'

'It's not as if he was going to keep his mouth shut if I didn't agree . . . But if he'd gone straight to the DCS, I'd have been left with a bent copper to black my sheet and that would have been curtains for promotion. I couldn't face that. So what does that make me?'

'Who wasn't going to keep his mouth shut? Who would have destroyed your chance of promotion?'

He told her.

'Poor man,' she said.

It was not the reaction he had expected. 'You can call him that when he worked with those bastards?'

'They blackmailed him into doing so.'

'Because he'd been screwing a tart when his wife was sick.'

'But he claims the woman set out to seduce him. Presumably, she's an expert?'

'I'd never have expected to hear you defend a man who's spat in his wife's bed.'

'I'm not defending, just trying to understand.'

'There's no understanding a traitor.'

'If I were in terrible trouble, wouldn't you forget all your principles if to do so would help me?'

He was silent for a long while, then he said: 'I wish I could say no; I can't.'

'Well then?'

'That doesn't alter anything. If I'd refused to work with him, he said he'd go to the DCS.'

'Can you be certain he would have done when he knew that there could be no way of persuading Mr Jameson to cooperate, so he was bound to be arrested and charged?'

'Of course I can't.'

'Suppose he was being completely honest. If Mr Jameson were handling the inquiries rather than you, would there be a better chance of finding the girl?'

'At this stage, no. It might even lessen them because more people would know what was happening and word might somehow leak out.'

'And saving her must be infinitely more important than saving your conscience?'

'That isn't why I agreed to work with Carr.'

'Does it really matter?'

He was no longer certain.

27

The list of silver Porsche 911s owned by people who lived in the given area was larger than either man had expected.

'All we can hope is that the bastards holding her aren't reckoning to move just yet,' Carr said.

Hoskin nodded. He did not find it easy to continue to work with Carr.

Carr made his way down to one of the interview rooms. There, he used the internal phone to ask WPC Gatling to collect all the local directories from the reference room and to join him.

When she arrived, she said, as she dropped the several directories on the table: 'Next time, you can collect the bloody things yourself.' The police force was still a man's world and, as did many women, she adopted a loud-mouthed, butch attitude in order to establish her equality.

He passed across a page of names and addresses. 'We need the telephone numbers of everyone on the list. If they're ex-directory, make a note and when we've finished, I'll take the names up to the DI and he'll get on to BT to ask for the numbers.'

She sat. 'What's all this in aid of?'

'We're trying to identify the owner of a silver Porsche.'

'Why?'

'To have a chat with him.'

'What about?'

'The kind of oil he uses in his car.'

'You lot in CID can't even tell the time without turning it into a mystery. Makes you feel important, does it?'

They finished the task at five-thirty. 'I'll take these upstairs,' he said, as he picked up the sheet of paper on which were the names and addresses of the nine owners whose telephone numbers were not listed.

'So I'll be on my way. You can return all the bloody books.' She stood.

'Hang on, we're not finished.'

'Maybe you aren't, but I am.'

'You want to argue it out with the super?'

She swore, fluently and not with imagination.

He was gone less than five minutes. When he returned, he had two phones and he plugged these into wall sockets. 'Start with the first number and ask to speak to the man of the house.'

'And say what? You want nice jog-jig, bargain offer, two quid and a packet of fags?'

'You're conducting a telephonic questionnaire to discover what is the most popular oil used in car engines.'

'Come on, it's too late in the day for joking.'

'No joke.'

'Since when have we carried out market research?'

'I'll be listening on the second phone to see if I can identify the voice.'

She spoke slowly. 'Mike, I have a feeling that this is something very big.'

'Then keep the feeling to yourself.'

'That makes a difference! Most of you randy bastards want me to hang 'em out in full view.'

She was intelligent, smart, and when not trying to prove herself to be macho, projected a warm personality. Despite the time and the nature of her call, she aroused cooperation rather than resentment. She learned that almost all drivers had no idea what oil was in their cars.

At eight, she said: 'Mike, it really is time to call a halt.

I'm hungry, thirsty, my voice is beginning to croak, and I've learned to hate engine oil.'

'Keep going a bit longer.'

She studied him. 'It's that important?'

He nodded.

'Something to do with the kidnapping?'

'Nothing.'

'I reckon you're lying. So I'll keep on until I either lose my voice or faint from hunger.'

She did not have to go to such lengths. At a quarter past eight, the man who answered the call said: 'Yes?'

'Mr Trent?'

'Well?'

'I'm conducting a survey on the oil you use in your car and I'd be most grateful for your help.'

'Do you know what the time is?'

Carr, his excitement all the stronger because he had begun to give up hope, recognized the voice.

'Indeed, and I must apologize for disturbing your evening. But, as you will know, husbands are at work during the day . . .' The line had gone dead. She replaced the receiver. 'Sorry about that, Mike.' Then she saw his expression. 'Jack the lad?'

He nodded.

'Thank God!'

Three minutes later, he stood in front of the D I's desk. 'You can tell B T we don't need those numbers after all. We've identified him.'

'How certain are you?'

'A hundred and one per cent.'

'What's the address?'

'Kingsley House, West Barton.'

Hoskin stood and crossed the room to study the large-scale map of the county which hung on the wall and which in addition to all normal features, showed the divisional boundaries. 'G division . . . D'you know the area?'

'Only very vaguely.'

He returned to the desk, leaned across to pick up the outside phone, dialled. 'Mrs Jameson, Hoskin speaking. Could I have a word with your husband . . . Yes, I know, but it is very important.' He put his hand over the mouthpiece. 'He must think he's the only man who arrives home shagged out.'

It was, Carr knew, a measure of the other's excitement that he had made that comment; normally, he would never have criticized a senior in front of a junior.

After a couple of minutes, Jameson demanded to know what was so important that his evening was interrupted.

'I think we may have a definite lead in the Lumley case, sir,' Hoskin said.

Jameson was a large man who recently had put on considerable weight. He had a round head, seemingly made rounder by growing baldness, and a heavily featured face which correctly suggested a quick temper.

Dressed in an old sweater and baggy corduroys, sheepskin-lined slippers on his feet, he stood in front of the fireplace in the sitting room of his home in north Rickstone. 'You should have informed me immediately the D C reported to you,' he said angrily.

'I thought . . .'

'The story headlined, every force in the country on red alert, Buckingham Palace asking to be kept informed, and you decide to play it solo. Bloody hell, your brains must shake around like loose marbles.'

'I considered the matter very carefully, sir, and came to the conclusion that since the evidence suggested the mob might have a lead through to someone in the force, all information needed to be kept as restricted as possible.'

Jameson's voice rose. 'And you reckoned I might be the grasser?'

'Hardly, sir. But by the very nature of your position, and the action you would be bound to be seen to take, a number of people would realize what was up. Having kept dead quiet until now, I can be certain that only D C Carr and I are aware of the facts.'

Jameson took time to consider the position. If the operation ended in failure, Hoskin would have to pay the penalty of his failure to observe the rules; but since it might well end in success, it had to be reasonable to let the problem slide for the moment.

Because of the identity of the victim, general cooperation was assured without any of the usual bureaucratic manoeuvring for position and even in technical breach of certain of the rules governing the surveillance of suspects. The land phone at Kingsley House was tapped and a scanner was set up to intercept any transmission from a mobile phone; experts, capable – with the aid of computer power – of decoding a message sent digitally, were put on stand-by. As soon as possible next morning, detectives visited local shops and pubs and very carefully, very discreetly, learned what they could about the occupants of the house. Because the land was flat and virtually without cover, watchers had to be set too far back to keep close watch on the house, but at least they were able to note all traffic moving, now that lanes were free enough of snow to be passable.

The RAF were called in. They overflew the house in a reconnaissance plane equipped with surveillance cameras, high enough for any uninformed watcher to believe it to be one more civilian airliner, low enough for the photographic resolution to be good. The photographs were developed and examined by expert analysts. In none of them was there anything visible that could confirm or deny that Angelique Lumley was being held in the house.

By dusk on Thursday, the police were in the position of knowing a little more than when they begun, but not nearly as much as they'd hoped. The house had been rented by Trent several months before from the owner who had had to let it following severe losses at Lloyds. He did not mix with the local inhabitants, although those who had briefly met him reported him to be pleasant and friendly. He seldom entertained and it had been noted that when he did, his guests were all male. He employed no indoor staff and only one part-time gardener. The gardener, treated to several drinks, gave it as his opinion that Mr Trent was nice enough, but not quality. And no, he'd not seen any ladies around the place recently – or in the past, for that much, but as far as he was concerned, a man's pleasures were his own business.

During the day, no phone call was either made or received.

It was clear that further action was necessary, yet this could not be so direct as to alert the occupants of the house to the fact that they were under suspicion. It was decided to take advantage of the dark. People often became careless then, believing themselves to be hidden. The Metropolitan police were asked for the loan of their helicopter which had recently been equipped with a Canadian designed and built night-time surveillance system. Two passes over the house were to be made so that all four sides could be viewed from a low angle, as opposed to the very high angle from the plane. If these flights were spaced as far apart in time as possible, it was hoped that the occupants of the house, if they noted them, would fail to find them significant. One was made just after eleven, the other at five in the morning.

At first viewing, the video recordings, seen as if shot through a ghostly green light, seemed to show nothing of any consequence. But on the third viewing, an eagle-eyed woman noticed something. The third and top floor was marked by small dormer windows, set back in the roof, and therefore back from the vertical line of the outside walls, which served the warren of rooms once used by servants. On the south-facing side, the windows were blank, but the fourth one looked as if curtains had been drawn across it. Computer enhancing technique was used to sharpen the images and it became clear that the curtains were in fact a crude form of boarding.

The ACC (Crime), chairman of the small committee, said: 'It could, of course, merely be a temporary repair and not there to blank out the window so that the person inside can't see out. Against that possibility, the boarding is on the inside, the experts are convinced the glazing is intact, and there are no signs of any damage which might call for temporary repairs. So now we have to decide on the answers to certain questions. Do we accept that the dormer window is boarded up because Miss Lumley is held captive in the room? If we can't be certain, do we take the risk of assuming that that is so? Do we then make a rescue attempt right away, or do we play it cautiously and try to gain more information, one way or another, remembering that it is virtually certain that the moment a ransom demand is made, events will move very, very quickly, perhaps too quickly for us to be able to respond with precision?'

They were silent; some sat still, some fidgeted. They had to make the decision, yet knew that if they got it wrong it would haunt them for a long time if she were not there, but was being held somewhere else . . . There was not at the moment the incriminating evidence necessary to warrant the arrest of Trent or, for that much, any of the others. So unless this could be found in the house – and if she were not being held captive there, and never had been, what was the likelihood of that? – they must remain free. In which case, Angelique would almost certainly be murdered in order to make certain that she could never incriminate them (however carefully her captors had concealed their identities from her, there had to be the possibility that while what she had learned could never imperil them when the police had no knowledge of who

173

they were, it most certainly could once they were singled out).

'I think we have to go in as soon as possible,' the ACC finally said.

One by one, they agreed.

28

Wyatt walked into Hoskin's room at eight-fifteen. 'They say the girl's been found?'

'We hope so, but can't be certain until the house has been searched.'

'And you provided the vital information?'

'Mike turned it up, I passed it on.'

'So I was right – he was working with them?'

'Yes.'

'Until I became suspicious, I'd have bet my life that whatever the pressures, he'd never have gone bent. I know things were tough, but, Christ, after Victoria Arkwright . . . What happens now?'

'There's a suggestion that an SAS team is being called in.'

'That's not what I meant. Has Mike been arrested?'

'No.'

'But . . . Surely you've already told the DCS?'

'Of course.'

'Then . . . What did he say?'

'He was annoyed because according to him I'd sidestepped God knows how many rules and regulations, but since things have worked out, he couldn't get too hot under the collar. It wasn't all that difficult to cool him down.'

'You're saying he knows Mike was working for the bastards, but hasn't slapped the cuffs on him?'

Hoskin sat back in his chair. 'Why should he do that?'

'For God's sake, Guv, who's gone round the twist, you or me?'

'I can only speak for myself . . . I explained how things have been. That Mike reported to me the moment they tried to put the black on him and I decided it would be worth making it seem he'd given in to them in the hopes that he'd learn something that would finger them.'

'But . . . but that's wrong. Until I told you, you'd no idea Mike had turned crook.'

'I knew when you spoke that he hadn't turned crook. But I had to conceal that fact because it was vital that only he and I knew what was going on. Now that things are out in the open, though, I can say that the fact I didn't take you into my confidence doesn't mean I didn't and don't have the fullest faith in you.'

Wyatt respected rank to a far greater degree than most and so normally accepted what his seniors said or did simply because they were his seniors. But there was a stubborn, puritanical streak in him that occasionally surfaced. 'I'm not a fool.'

'You would not be my sergeant if you were.'

'When I told you I suspected Mike was working with the kidnapping mob, you wouldn't accept the possibility to begin with. So what's happened? Has Mike admitted everything on condition that you help him and you've agreed to that because the news of a copper in E division who's so bent he's worked with the kidnapping bastards would mean the end of any chance of promotion for you?'

'Are you calling me a liar?'

'I'm saying . . .' He became silent.

'You're accusing me of being so intent on promotion that in pursuit of it I'm willing to pervert the course of justice.' He paused, then said: 'Years ago, I knew a PC who accused his inspector of taking small bribes. When he failed to prove his allegation, he was dismissed from the force. It is obviously my duty to report to Detective Chief Superintendent Jameson the allegation you have just made. It is, of course, a far more serious allegation than that of taking small bribes and if you cannot provide the proof to sustain it, you'll obviously find yourself in very serious trouble . . . I like to think that I judge every man in the round, not the part. Therefore, provided I hear no more about it, I am willing to remember the quality of your past work and to put this ridiculous allegation down to the stress under which we've all been working.'

After a while, Wyatt left.

The assistant chief constable was officially in charge of operations, but everyone knew that it was the SAS lieutenant, an expert in hostage situations, who was responsible for planning. H-hour was to be dawn when the rescuers could see what they were doing and the men in the house would probably still be either asleep or in a state of drowsiness. The police, in six cars, would approach from two directions; those coming in from the south would have to cross a ten-acre field and then the garden, those from the north could drive up to the front door, so they would be synchronizing their movements to make certain they arrived at the house at exactly the same moment. The SAS team would be dropping in.

At the final briefing, the ACC made a point of reminding all present that no matter how appalling had been the cruelty of the mob, only the minimum of force was to be used.

For once, a plan worked without a single glitch. As the two teams of policemen arrived at the house, the four SAS men abseiled from the helicopter to land on the small ledge at the edge of the roof. With the agility of monkeys, they smashed their way through a dormer window, raced across the small, dust-laden room and out into the corridor.

They carried very high-powered torches and in the beams of these they saw a man in an armchair, clearly just awakened and trying to make sense of what was happening. As they came forward, they blinded him with the light. The lieutenant had a four-year-old daughter. 'No violence!' he shouted, as he kicked the man off the chair and on to the floor with sufficient force to fracture a shin bone. The sergeant had a two-year-old daughter. 'You heard!' he shouted, as he pulled the man up by his hair, then kneed him violently in the groin. Neither of the other two had children, but that didn't stop them adding their comments.

There was a key in the lock of the door by the chair. The lieutenant turned it and opened the door. On the bed lay a young, terrified woman.

'It's all right,' the lieutenant said. 'You're safe.'

For several seconds she dare not hope that this was for real. When she accepted that it was, largely because of the grins of unalloyed pleasure of the four, she burst into tears of relief.

Wyatt cursed himself for a coward. He knew what he should do, yet hesitated to do it.

But was it really that straightforward? Where was the proof? The significance of the facts which had led him to the conclusion that Mike was a traitor had been neutralized by the DI's claim of cooperation from the beginning. Without proof, it would be his word against theirs. Superior rank carried superior clout. Yet justice would be in poor shape if it were never pursued when there could be doubt; idealism would be castrated if no man was prepared to face heavy odds to do what he considered to be right . . .

What were the odds? Had the story of the PC who'd been kicked out of the force for making allegations against his superior that could not be proved been mere fiction? Wasn't it very much more reasonable to believe that a disciplinary hearing would have administered a severe reprimand? Yet he couldn't be certain. And it might be that for a detective sergeant to make so serious an unproven allegation against his detective inspector undermined discipline to such an extent that it would be held that dismissal from the force was the only suitable punishment. And if he were sacked? Immediate loss of income and possible future loss of pension. The mortgage on the house had several years to go and without a police pension he would be unable to meet the monthly repayments. Social security might meet them for a while, but not forever; and if the present political atmosphere was any guide, perhaps soon not at all. If the house were repossessed, Freda would be devastated. Only the death of one of her children could cause her greater emotional pain . . .

There were men brave enough – selfish enough? – to put their own and their loved ones' future in jeopardy in pursuit of truth and justice, but he was discovering that he was not one of them.

Jameson had a blunt, often loud manner, which tended to hide the fact that he was sharply intelligent. In shirt and braces – the heating was always unnecessarily high at county HQ – he rested his elbows on the desk. Eyes slightly hooded by fleshy eyebrows, he studied Hoskin, who had not been asked to sit. 'I've called you here because Trent has suggested he's open to a deal for pleading guilty; claimed that he could offer us some information that we'd find interesting if we agreed.'

'An admission in the Arkwright case?' Hoskin asked.

He ignored the question. 'We told him, no deal. In the end, he gave us the information anyway. He claims he photographed Carr screwing a high-class tart and used the photos to blackmail him into feeding information.'

'Which is what I reported to you.'

'His dates don't agree with yours.'

'Then his are wrong.'

'He says he started blacking Carr long before you claim Carr reported what was happening.'

'Anything to cause trouble.'

'Where's the woman?'

'She's disappeared.'

'Have you tried to find her?'

'Yes, without success. The only lead we've unearthed says she's gone abroad; there's no indication where.'

'Trent will talk in court how he was blackmailing Carr long before you knew anything.'

'If prosecuting counsel is out of knee-length shorts, he'll make Trent look the liar he is.'

'There's something else.'

'Which is?'

'Trent swears he paid three thousand in cash to Carr for information received. If Carr was working to your orders, he should have passed that on to you. You've given me no record that he did.'

'Because the three thousand is another figment of Trent's revengeful imagination.'

'Perhaps Carr received it, but didn't pass it on to you?'

'If he'd ever received a penny, he'd have passed it on.'

'You can't be certain.'

'I know my man. The only evidence of any extra spending on Carr's part is that in the last weeks of his wife's pregnancy, he moved her to a nursing home. The total bill there came to roughly two thousand five hundred. He told me he borrowed the money from his mother and when I had a word with her, she confirmed this.'

'I see.'

There was a silence. 'Is that all?' Hoskin asked.

'Yes.'

'There's not to be any apology?'

'For what?'

'For obviously having doubts about my D C's and my honesty just because of what a murdering bastard claims.'

'All such allegations have to be examined.'

'But not with such relish.'

'That's enough.'

Hoskin left. As the door closed, Jameson opened the top right drawer of the desk and brought out a packet of cheroots. Goddamnit, why couldn't he accept what he'd been told? Why did he have to question, when to do so must cause dangerous trouble? He'd not be further promoted before he retired, so he'd nothing to gain. Nothing, that was, except the knowledge that he'd retired knowing he had always pursued the truth, the whole truth, and nothing but the truth.

Timothy had been fed and was asleep in the nursery. Carr and Gloria faced each other in the sitting room. 'Would you . . .?' She plucked at the belt of her dress. 'Would you have told me if you hadn't been forced to because it'll come out in court?'

He said miserably: 'I wish I could honestly say yes, but . . .'

'But probably you wouldn't have done?'

'I knew how much it would hurt you.'

'But you didn't seem to know that when you were with her.'

'I wish I could explain. I can't. All I can say is, if she hadn't made all the running . . . But that's no excuse.'

They became silent.

'Mike. If they hadn't used that woman to blackmail you into helping them, would you ever have been able to work out where they were holding Angelique Lumley?'

'No.'

'And she would have suffered as horribly as Victoria Arkwright?'

'And probably have been murdered.'

'So she was saved because you . . . you went with that woman?'

'I suppose you could look at it like that.'

'Then that's how I will look at it. Makes my hurt so very less important.'

When he'd married her, he thought with deep humility, he'd been the luckiest of men.

The chief constable's suite, furnished in London clubland style, was on the seventh floor and consisted of an outer office, a much larger inner office, a seldom used bedroom, and a bathroom.

The CC's secretary, known as Frosty for reasons that were obvious if one accepted that thin lips were indicative of character, ushered Jameson into the inner office. The chief constable, who'd been standing out on the small balcony guarded by wrought-iron railings, stepped back into the room. "Morning.' He was a handsome man in his mid fifties, adept at saying and doing the right thing at the right time.

'Sorry to interrupt you, sir, but I . . .'

The chief constable interrupted him without any apology. 'I've just had a phone call. A very unexpected one.'

'Really, sir?' The chief constable's manner was so ebullient, and therefore out of character, that Jameson wondered if he had been drinking.

'It was to inform me . . .' He crossed to his desk and sat. He rested his elbows on the desk and stared into the distance. 'It was to inform me,' he said, speaking slowly and with emphasis, 'that the Royals are extremely grateful to me for having rescued Miss Lumley unharmed. They offer me their sincere congratulations. In addition, and as a mark of their gratitude, they propose to award me a knighthood. As I said, that will honour the whole county force, not just me.'

Bloody hypocrite, Jameson thought sourly. The other's wife must be in her seventh heaven. She was such a dedicated snob that probably she was already rehearsing how to react when the rank and file bowed and curtsied to her.

The chief constable coughed.

Jameson pulled himself together. 'Congratulations, sir.'

'Thank you. But, of course, we must not waste any more time on nonessentials. You wanted a word?'

'Yes, sir. Trent has made certain accusations against a member of the force.'

'Regretfully, to be expected.'

'I decided it was necessary to discuss these accusations in some detail with Inspector Hoskin.'

'And now they can be dismissed?'

'Not quite.'

'Why not?'

'There are a couple of points which do raise questions.'

'What are they?'

'I've compared the dates which Inspector Hoskin has given me with those which Trent has provided. They don't match. Trent claims to have started to blackmail Carr some time before Inspector Hoskin says Carr first came to him to report. Trent further claims –'

'What does Hoskin say?'

'He is certain his dates are correct.'

'Which is what one would expect when a detective inspector is logging events. I'm surprised you feel it worthwhile raising the point.'

'I wouldn't have done if there weren't something more. Trent further claims he sent Carr three thousand pounds in the post as payment. Inspector Hoskin states that Carr has never made any reference to this money.'

'Which makes it clear that the money is a figment of Trent's malign imagination.'

'But Inspector Hoskin told me that he had checked for any unusual expenditure. He found that Carr had moved his wife from hospital into a nursing home and the bill was roughly two thousand five hundred. Carr's explanation as to how he could afford that was that his mother had lent him the money; the mother confirmed the fact.'

'Which surely puts an end to that?'

'But if Carr had been working with Inspector Hoskin

from the beginning, why would Hoskin have been looking for unaccounted spending on Carr's part before Trent's accusation was made? Obviously, there are two possible answers. This check was an insurance; covering the possibility that the allegation would be made in court as an attempt at revenge. Secondly, that when Hoskin checked, he had reason to be suspicious in which case, of course, Carr had not reported to him and they were not working together, even though Carr had started to cooperate with the mob.

'Obviously, we must ascertain which is the correct answer. I suggest the easiest way of doing that is to examine the financial affairs of Mrs Carr and determine if there is any trace of the three thousand pounds she claims to have lent him.'

The chief constable stared into the distance for a long time. Then he said: 'If one were to carry out such a search, it would be emotionally very painful for Mrs Carr, not only because it would be calling her a liar, but also because it would show that we are considering the possibility of her son being a criminal.'

'Our work often causes pain.'

'Tell me something. Does the answer to these questions have any bearing on the case against Trent and his accomplices?'

'It cannot affect the verdict, no, sir.'

'Then what would be gained by pursuing the matter?'

Jameson showed his surprise. 'If Carr was blackmailed into becoming a traitor and Hoskin uncovered this fact, but did not report it . . .'

'There are times, Mark, when it is kinder to some to take a pragmatic approach and let arcane possibilities lie fallow. I think this is one such time.'

'Are you saying we shouldn't check out Mrs Carr's financial affairs, despite the possibility that . . .'

'I think so.'

Jameson waited for an explanation. There was none.

'Thank you,' said the chief constable.

It was only when Jameson was in the lift that he overcame his bewilderment sufficiently to understand. If it were proved that Carr had been blackmailed into cooperating with the mob and that Hoskin had discovered this fact but far from reporting it, as was his duty, had with calculated design hidden it, then the resulting story, in a case that had already gained intense publicity, would feed the media's headlines for days on end. A knighthood could hardly be awarded to the chief constable to honour a force that was shown to be so corrupted. Deprived of her 'Lady', his wife would be a very bitter woman indeed . . .